QUADROPHOBIA

SHAUN QUINN

Copyright © 2014 Shaun Quinn

Quadrophobia is a work of fiction. Any resemblance between the characters that appear in these pages and actual persons, living or dead, is purely coincidental.

All rights reserved. No part of this publication may be reproduced, stored in a retrieval system, or transmitted in any form or by any means, electronic, mechanical, photocopying, recording or otherwise, without the prior permission of the copyright owner.

Cover photo: © Shutterstock/Peter Gudella

CreateSpace Independent Publishing Platform

ISBN: 1500361631

ISBN-13: 978-1500361631

To my family

Monday
39 years, 359 days

I woke this morning and realised that I'm going to turn 40 in a week's time. Sunday 24th August. I wasn't exactly oblivious of the fact that I'm already 39 and in my 40th year, but the past 12 months have been so busy that time has literally flown by. I thought I had at least a fortnight left, but this is my last week. Shit! It's nearly here—the big four-zero.

There's actually less than a week left, as today is Monday and my birthday's on Sunday. But I was born late in the evening, so I've technically got one of each of the days of the week left until I officially turn 40. I'm glad I remembered in time. I need to prepare myself; I need to think; I need to reflect; I need to do certain things. It's going to be a busy week...

I hate Mondays at the best of times. I never seem to feel relaxed after the weekend. Isn't that what weekends are for–relaxing? I always end up doing far too much. It's less of a time to wind down and more of a time to catch up on the stuff that couldn't be done during the week, like tidying the house, paying bills and fixing broken things. The kids have to be taken to their activities; the shopping needs doing; the car needs cleaning; the garden needs tending to, etc. etc. Add an outing or a social event to the list of duties and I end up well and truly fucked. Well, *we* end up fucked, as Fiona helps with the multitude of chores that stack up during the week and need attending to on weekends–though mostly it's me that gets them done.

This Monday morning felt like no other. I slept pretty poorly last night. Once the kids were finally in bed, Fiona and I shared a bottle of wine and watched a film. It was nice to spend some quality time together. I'd hoped that we'd make love. But we started arguing for no reason, which put a stop to that. I said some things that I shouldn't have. So did she. We eventually went to bed at 1:00am, after which I couldn't get to sleep. I was wound up and my mind wouldn't switch off.

It struck me, during my trudge to the train station this morning, how damn tired I've become over the last few years. Commuting into London has ground me down. After the birth of Michael, our tiny flat in Elephant and Castle became too restrictive, so we opted for a quieter life and a more sizeable house, in rural Essex. The flip-side is the long, expensive commute. I've now been traveling for nearly three hours a day, for two years straight.

As I'd not commuted before, I was at first pretty shocked by the ragged look of some of my fellow passengers, who it seemed had been worn down by the early rise and the daily travel. I'm now one of these people–stern faced robots, performing the same joyless routine in silence; reluctantly making the pilgrimage to work or desperately trying to get home at the end of the day.

The worse part has to be the Underground. I literally dread going down that hole in the earth. The scene on a Monday morning is truly grim–hundreds of faceless, agitated souls crammed into a stinky, sweaty, creaking box, rattling its way through an ancient sewer system, deep beneath the city.

Some mornings, usually, but not exclusively Mondays, I feel like 45 going on 50, such is the low level of energy available in my body to drag me out of bed and in to work. It's worst in winter–leaving the house in the dark, waiting on an icy platform and listening to the coughs and splutters, as the latest strain of virus spreads around the carriage.

One plus side of weekday mornings is breakfast with the kids. They still rise early, full of energy and with smiles on their faces. Suzy is six and Michael is three. As I'm first up, I take them downstairs, leaving Fiona to sleep for another half hour or so. We feed the cat, who's already meowing for her food. The kids stroke her or dance around the kitchen to the radio, while I fix breakfast. Then, sitting there in our pyjamas, we eat and talk. They always want to try different toast toppings. Currently they're into peanut butter with chocolate spread. It's far too sweet for me, but they love it. I stick to marmite instead, which goes better with the earthy taste of my morning coffee.

Those bleary-eyed minutes that we spend together at the beginning of each day are so important for our relationship. I try to make them laugh or I explain things to them, perhaps something mentioned on the radio. I also share my thoughts.

This morning I announced to the kids that I'm going to be 40 in a week's time. Suzy, who can now count up to one hundred, said "Wow", though with little conviction. Michael has only a basic concept of numbers, but asked "Are you really old Daddy?" I had to admit that yes, I am.

Our breakfast ritual has to be perfectly timed in order for me to make my train. The kids' only duty is to eat their food and not fight with each other, which they mostly manage to do. I glance at the clock on the oven every now and then to check how we are progressing. I need to finish my breakfast by 6.45am. I then leave them to continue on their own, while I head upstairs to get dressed and clean my teeth. By this time Fiona is usually up and goes downstairs to take over.

She was still in bed, in the dark, when I entered the bedroom this morning. She stirred and started to get up. She looked like she'd also slept badly. I suddenly remembered last night. It was depressing.

The room smelt awful, so I opened a window. I felt a little repulsed. It was partly the sight of Fiona waking up, partly the morning odour in our room, but mostly to do with how I was currently feeling about myself...and about us.

She went into our en-suite and closed the door, so I cleaned my teeth in the main bathroom, using an old toothbrush that had been left behind by a visitor. Then I headed back downstairs. The kids had finished their breakfast and Suzy was helping Michael put his cereal bowl on the sideboard. I gave them a kiss, told them that Mummy was running late and sent them upstairs to see her.

Then I did something I've not done before...I left the house without saying goodbye to Fiona. I was already running late and I simply couldn't face her this morning. I was still pissed off about last night.

It was a surprisingly chilly day for August. The summer's been very poor so far, with perhaps only a week of decent sunny weather back in July. Everyone's already dressed in coats, as if they've given up on the summer ever happening. If August's meant to be the hottest month of the year, and we're now over half way through it, then it's surely downhill weather-wise from now?

My thoughts were as grey as the overcast sky as I walked to the station. It was a poor start to the last week of my 30's; I already felt crap in body and mind.

The trains to London were screwed up and it looked like there were people still waiting for the previous service. The automated announcement blamed it on a broken-down unit further up the line, as if it was somebody else's fault, then added "We apologise for any inconvenience to your journey." The chap beside me swore under his breath.

The late-running 6:55am finally rumbled in and we squeezed into the available standing space. I stood by the door as the train rocked its way to the next provincial station to pick up more drab, pissed-off commuters. I caught a glimpse of myself in the shabby, scratched glass. I looked tired and depressed. The curvature of the window accentuated the size of my forehead, so I appeared bald. I had black lines beneath my eyes, which contrasted against my pale, sun-deprived skin. It wasn't a pleasant sight.

The train stopped at a large town just outside London and a few people got off. I was quick enough to grab one of the vacated seats. I slumped down and closed my eyes.

I often doze off on the train—that's if I'm lucky enough to find somewhere to sit. I try to carry on where I stopped an hour earlier when my alarm woke me. Some days I get an extra half hour or so and I feel a little more energised when the train arrives in the city. This morning I couldn't get back to sleep. Instead, I just sat and looked out the window, thinking about the significance of the week ahead of me.

If I've only one week left, then what do I want to do with it? What do I want to achieve? Is there something I need to change? What did I forget to do so far in my 30's?

I couldn't think of much. I just want to feel less tired, less old, more energetic and more youthful. I want to work less and have fewer responsibilities. I want not to be turning 40, as all the things that I hate in my life come with the territory. I'm no longer a young man, full of energy, free of pressures, enjoying life and thinking only about myself. Those days ended a long time ago in the blur of my 30's, during which I got married, bought a house, had kids and started working far too much in order to keep up with the demands of 21st century life. Perhaps it's futile to fight the gradual and inevitable slide into middle age? What difference is a week going to make anyway?

Then I remembered something that I want, besides more free time, a replacement body and a younger, sexier wife...

Money.

It's something that I never seem to have enough of. I don't want to be super-rich or even just affluent, as that surely has its own drawbacks—like turning into a wanker. I just want to not worry about money and not to be in debt. I want to have some savings and to be able to splash out once in a while. The situation that Fiona and I have found ourselves in is that our incomings almost exactly equal our outgoings—well there must be a slight imbalance, as we are slowly creeping into the red and we don't have the means to pay off what is a rather modest, but persistent overdraft.

I recently totted up our finances in order to work out where our money goes each month. It wasn't an easy task. The first problem was recognising which companies are responsible for each of the multitude of direct debits that chip away at our salaries. I was unable to positively identify a few. One seemed to be instalments for a fridge we bought years ago and are still paying off. Another mystery direct debit was from an insurance company that I was sure we were no longer with. I called the buggers up, to get the bottom of it. To my horror I was informed that they'd sent a letter at the end of the first year, kindly notifying us that we could "Sit back and relax", as they would continue to provide cover. Apparently, we'd needed to contact them to stop the policy being automatically renewed. I demanded to have it cancelled immediately, but they wanted me to pay the rest of the year's balance. I couldn't believe it! I eventually snapped and called them "Fucking leaches", then slammed the phone down. We're still paying the damn thing.

After that, I went through our various policies, contracts, agreements, protection plans, etc. etc. and tried to identify those that we're paying to much too for and those that we can do without. This involved many hours queuing on the telephone, listening to various annoying repeating jingles and talking to call centre operators of all ages and nationalities, who tried to persuade me to stay with their particular company. In the end, the overall saving on our monthly budget was minuscule. We've still got very little room to manoeuvre.

If I'm going to whither away traveling into London and back, and go blind from staring at a computer screen, then I want to be more handsomely compensated for it. That way I can enjoy the few hours a day that I have with my wife and kids in the knowledge that we are saving at least a little each month. We might then be able to afford a summer holiday on a more regular basis. I could perhaps call in a builder, a plumber or a decorator to do stuff to the house, rather than bodging repairs and renovations myself. I could treat Fiona and the kids on a whim, without assessing the possibility of gift-giving in the light of forthcoming expenses.

Overall, I just want to feel relaxed about money. It bothers me too much.

A possible opportunity to achieve this particular goal is coming up later in the week. The boss has invited interested parties to pitch for a sizeable project that the company is taking on. We specialise in the design, installation and monitoring of fire protection and emergency systems. Our clients are mostly small to medium-sized businesses and domestic properties, but we've recently won the contract for a hospital in Birmingham that's going to be renovated. The job is huge by our standards. It will be planned and managed by a single team, who will focus almost entirely on the project for a year. This will mean plenty of overtime pay for the lucky crew that get it, plus an attractive package for the team leader. Though I don't fancy traveling to

Birmingham regularly, nor staying up there once a week, which will be necessary, at least during the initial phase of the project, the chance of a promotion is very tempting. I've not gotten a pay rise in three years, so this could be my chance.

I've already expressed an interest in the project and been up to the site with Darius, a trainee on my team, to scout out the job. This involved a particularly enjoyable beer and curry session. We've made some notes, which I need to turn into a concrete plan. I'm due to present our proposal on Friday, when senior management will decide who gets it.

On account of the size of the job, there's only one other team pitching for it. This is led by Terry Francis, or 'Twatface', as Darius and I call him. TF is an arrogant, pushy, self-confident prat, who in his short time with the firm has brown-nosed, blagged and cheated his way from a Trainee to Applications Team Leader—a progression that's taken me nearly 15 years. I wouldn't mind TF so much if he was genuinely talented and knew his stuff, even half as well as I do, but the man is at least 50% bullshit, from the way he works, to the way he carries on at the office—bragging and goading colleagues, and sliming the womenfolk. He seems to have it in for me of late and has become a bit of a nemesis. The rest of his team aren't much better. Some of them used to be colleagues. Twatface has turned them into little versions of himself.

The thought of TF and his team getting the Birmingham project fills me with dread and panic. If they get chosen over us then we'll look shit. The worse thing though is that he'll then be at a higher level than me, and on a better salary. He'll be more senior, despite having been at the firm for less than half the time. I would see it every day in his eyes and his smirky grin. It would make coming into work worse than it already is. If Twatface continues at the same rate that he's risen so far through the company, then he might even make senior management in a couple more years. Then I'll be working under him. That would be hell!

I was going through this horrible scenario as I made my dreary way along the Tube, swinging from the handrail, in close confinement with a bunch of other anonymous people, all rubbing against each other. It brought on a bout of heartburn. I reached for an indigestion tablet from the stash I always keep in my bag. I was already stressed out and it was only Monday morning. I'd not even made it into work.

My thoughts turned briefly to Fiona. I'd expected her to text me. I knew she'd be upset, or perhaps pissed off that I left without saying goodbye. As I emerged from the Underground and my phone once more found a signal, there was still no word from her. I concluded that she was pissed off.

Work was as shit as always. I battled with my mass of emails, deleting the spam, responding immediately to a few urgent ones and leaving a handful in my ever-growing inbox, for a later date. I recently tried checking my email just twice a day–half an hour in the morning and half an hour in the afternoon–but this approach didn't really work, as it's not enough time to deal with the deluge of messages that find their way to me each day. Also, certain things need responding to immediately, so I missed a few important emails from clients and the directors. For that reason, I've gone back to keeping my account open all day.

After breaking the back of my daily electronic postbag, I checked on the other members of the team. Only Clare and Darius were in the office, as Mark and Ryan were out on site. Clare, as always, looked rather sprightly for a Monday morning. She was wearing her trouser-suit outfit. She always dresses in either a trouser-suit or a skirt-suit. I prefer the skirt version on account of her nice legs. She smiled and sat upright, then without me asking, filled me in on what she was doing. It's hard to fault Clare. She's efficient, reliable, pleasant and presentable—a real credit to the team.

Darius on the other hand is a bit of a pikey and a slacker. He's neither efficient nor reliable, nor is he particularly presentable. However, he's very funny and he's good at drinking beer. These are also important qualities.

Darius was blatantly surfing the web, checking the weekend's footy news, He greeted me with a nonchalant "What's up." I asked if he'd had any further ideas about the Birmingham project over the weekend. He looked at me disapprovingly, then proceeded to fill me in on something he'd heard on the way to work...

Apparently TF had been on the same bus as him, sitting a few seats away. He was on the phone to someone, claiming that he's "...more or less secured the promotion." Darius was sure that was what he'd said. It was exactly what I did *not* want to hear. I asked if TF had seen him, in case it was a joke. He wasn't sure.

Perhaps it's true? I wouldn't be surprised if TF has struck a deal with the boss. Promotions are often decided in advance, making the interview a false and rather pointless exercise. Though if his team have already been awarded the job, then he surely wouldn't be stupid enough to mouth off about it, would he? Perhaps it was just a wind up, to put me off for Friday? I wouldn't put it past him.

By lunchtime I was truly blue. It was one of the worst starts to a week ever.

In summer I usually eat on one of the benches in the plaza, adjacent to our office block. But it was raining outside, so I sat at my desk and had a sandwich instead. I couldn't bear to go into the coffee room. If the rumour about Birmingham is true then it would've been far too humiliating.

Fiona had still not texted, emailed or called. Either she was genuinely upset or she was also playing hard-to-get after last night. I eventually started to wonder if she was alright. This quickly turned into genuine worry, so I gave in and called her. There was no answer.

I couldn't concentrate in the afternoon. Neither Darius nor Clare needed me, so I sat in front of my computer and once more attempted to shift my backlog of emails. Most of them required too much brainpower and patience to deal with, which I guess is why they'd remained unanswered for so long. In there was the original message from the boss, announcing the Birmingham project. I'd more or less accepted that I'm not going to get it, so I deleted the email.

Luckily no one called, as I wasn't in the right frame of mind to deal with anything.

At afternoon coffee break I went outside to the plaza to try Fiona again. After two attempts she picked up the phone. She didn't sound pleased to hear from me. I offered an apology for this morning. She brushed it off, as if she hadn't noticed. She then said she was busy and had to go, so she hung up.

Walking back into the building, I passed TF in the corridor. He was the last person I wanted to see at that moment. He was with one of his crew. I dropped my head and tried to avoid eye contact. He didn't say anything...He didn't need to. Just having to pass by him at that moment was enough. He'd won. I accepted the inevitable—that I'm about to be pipped by someone more confident, energetic and savvy, who's nearly 10 years my junior.

I left work at five on the dot, without saying goodbye to anyone. I took the side exit, as I couldn't even face the receptionist. The train ride home was as depressing as always. I suspected that I was heading back for an argument with Fiona.

When I finally got in I just wanted to slump on the sofa, take off my sweaty socks and have a coffee. Instead, Fiona announced that she was off for a jog with her friend, so I needed to look after the kids. She was already in the hall, in her trainers, leggings and a sweat-top. She rolled her eyes at me and jogged on out of the house, leaving me to close the door behind her.

The kids were in the kitchen, where I'd left them in the morning. They were eating dinner this time—spaghetti bolognese. They smiled at me and I went in for a kiss. It was just what I needed at the end of a particularly shit Monday, despite the cold slimy sauce on their chops.

I sat with them and asked them about their day. Suzy couldn't recall too much of school, except "Playing in the playground." Michael had been at nursery for most of the day. Heaven knows what he gets up to there. I've never visited. It's not possible given that I work 45 miles away in London. It seems wrong that I know more about the damn plaza outside my office than I do of the little world that he inhabits for five hours a day. It would be lovely to see him playing with the toys, interacting with the other children, exploring, learning and developing as a person.

This has to be something I need to rectify–my absence from my children's life. We only get to spend breakfast and dinner together during the week, before they head off to bed. If I could only drop them off to school or pick them up at the end of the day, it would make life much more bearable. The promotion that I'm after will involve working even more and traveling further, so it'll surely mean even less time with the kids. What a conundrum!

By the time I'd gotten Suzy and Michael to bed and read them a story, Fiona was back from her jog. She made herself a salad and disappeared into the study. I stuck a frozen pizza in the oven and opened a beer. I try not to drink on Mondays, so that I've at least one alcohol-free day per week, but it'd been such a shit day and I needed something to sedate me.

Fiona and I ignored each other for most of evening. The house is large enough. I watched TV in the lounge, hoping that she'd eventually come in and join me. She sat in front of the computer in the study, probably surfing the Web. I didn't go in to see her either.

I heard her go up to bed at 11:00pm. I was still in a bad mood and feeling insecure. I was trying to act as if I don't care that *she* doesn't seem to care about me, so I watched a little more crap on the box. I contemplated sleeping on my own, on the sofa bed in the spare room, but then I thought better of it.

I went upstairs around midnight. Fiona was already fast asleep.

Tuesday
39 years, 360 days

I absolutely did *not* want to go in to work this morning. I slept poorly again and woke with a sore throat. It felt like I was coming down with something, so I took some paracetamol just in case. I live on the things in winter, to stave off illness. It works most of the time, until my immune system finally gives in and I'm struck down with an almighty flu. This felt like a mere minnow of a virus, so I'm sure the pills will see it off. I'd rather have stayed in bed though.

Though Monday is my least favourite day of the week, Tuesdays aren't normally that much better. After just one day into the working week I'm already knackered, having used up any energy that I managed to store up during the weekend. Yesterday took a lot out of me, so there was very little wind in my sails as I began the day. Even the kids' morning antics failed to perk me up.

Scarlet takes the train on Tuesdays, which adds some interest to the commute, if I see her. She's a particularly hot passenger—a bit of eye candy for us men. Her name's probably not Scarlet, that's just what I call her. She might be Elaine or Janice to some other guy. She wasn't at the station, in her usual spot by the disused grey ticket booth. I've not seen her for a couple of weeks. Pity.

I see the same people on the platform every day. Their faces, their patterns and their behaviour are so familiar to me, like they're old friends or family members, yet I've never spoken to any of them and nor do I know who they are, or what they do for a living. There's the old guy who reads two newspapers—one broadsheet and one free paper; there's the well-dressed, dark-haired woman who gets dropped off by her husband on Wednesdays; there's the slightly scruffy and underdressed office lad who always consumes an energy drink in the morning and hides at the end of the platform for a sneaky cigarette.

I sometimes spot some of my fellow commuters around the village on weekends. It's difficult to know what to do. Should I say hello, or should I just ignore them as I do every day on the platform? We normally make eye contact, perhaps nod, but never go any further. I tried sparking up conversation with one or two people at the station when we first moved to the area. I'd assumed that's how one behaves outside of London. But I was wrong. People are slightly more approachable, but the train station is still eerily quiet on weekday mornings. Everyone is already in 'commuter-mode'–guarded, steely, selfish and ready for a day's mission in the Capital. I quickly conformed to this norm, though the lack of basic human kindness still depresses me.

The daily rush for seats is a particularly shameful ritual that I resent being a part of, yet one that I find myself participating in. The early train is massively overcrowded, so unless you can afford to travel in first class, there's fierce competition for a spot by the time it reaches the station. It's as if we're already in London the moment the doors open. Everyone piles in and heads straight for the few available seats. This perhaps explains why no one talks to each other on the platform. It's dog-eat-dog, survival of the fittest, each man and woman for his and her self.

I guess the morning jostle is to be expected given that there are more people than seats. One thing I can't stand, however, is 'seat-hogging'–that is the taking up of two seats at busy times. Seat-hoggers generally get on the train further up the line, where it's less crowded. They therefore feel that it's their right to occupy two adjacent pews. They reserve their extra seat with a bag or coat and only vacate it when asked to do so by another passenger. Of course most people are too shy to ask, or are simply too cocooned in commuter-mode to interact with another human being, even if it might save them standing up for 50 minutes. Seat-hogs are well aware of this and use it to their advantage to create a buffer between themselves and other travellers.

Other seat-hoggers employ a slightly less obvious strategy–sitting by the aisle and leaving the window seat beside them free. This approach also relies on people's reluctance to speak up. In the event that another passenger asks to use the vacant seat, which happens relatively infrequently, they simply get up and let them sit by the window, then sit down again on the aisle seat, thus maintaining at least a partial barrier from human contact on one side.

The worst type of seat-hogger combines the above two techniques—occupying the window seat with their bag or coat and sitting by the aisle themselves. This usually ensures that no one denies them their god-given right to two seats. In the selfish world of train commuting, they are the ultimate breed of self-centred individual. They have no qualms about making their fellow man or woman stand in order to gain extra space. They're in it only for themselves. They're the Twatface of commuting. Basically cunts.

I've not told Fiona about TF and the Birmingham job yet. We barely spoke last night and all I said to her this morning was "Morning" and "Bye." She'll be really disappointed if I don't get the promotion. She's got her eye on a new kitchen. With the extra income, we'll be able to take out a smallish loan to afford one. We've been to look at a few that she likes and I know her mind's now made up. I don't agree that a kitchen should be our priority, as the current one is in a fair state, though it couldn't exactly be described as 'modern'. Ever since she saw our friends' swish new installation she's wanted to change ours. I foolishly made some encouraging noises, which she took to indicate my full endorsement of the project. Now there's no turning back. It's new kitchen or bust!

Fiona definitely changed once Michael was born. We agreed that we'd stop after two children. She'd been desperate to have kids, once we got married, but it took some years for her to fall pregnant. A year after Suzy was born the feeling came back in a strong way, but again, we didn't manage to conceive straight away, which caused more stress and anxiety.

During our attempts to produce Michael, I insisted that we don't have a third child, as I can't stand to go through the whole process again—it took so much out of both of us and affected our relationship. I was therefore relived when he came and we could call it a day.

Despite the upheaval of the first year or two I felt that he made our family complete—one girl, one boy; big sister and little brother. It appeared that Fiona felt the same, but she then became restless and unsatisfied. At first, I wasn't sure why. But I'm increasingly of the impression that she is missing something—the baby cycle. I could be wrong, but I feel that she might still have the urge. Given that we agreed to stop at two, which I still hope we do, this could explain her often desperate need for certain material items that her friends have, such as a new kitchen. I'm no female psychologist, but I think this is where it stems from...She also seems to resent me more of late, though that's a whole other subject entirely.

On arriving at the office, Clare asked me if I'd been OK yesterday. My sudden departure hadn't gone unnoticed. She seemed to be enquiring about my physical health rather than my mental state, so I informed her that I'd felt a bit queasy, but that I was better now. She smiled at me, as if she was happy that I'd recovered. Clare is very caring like that. She had her trouser-suit on again.

    I dealt with my mass of emails as per usual and answered a few old messages that I'd not had the courage to tackle yesterday. One was from Clive Nestor, a wealthy client who lives in Chislehurst. We're kitting out his home with a state-of-the-art fire protection system. He has a rather opulent detached property situated off the main road through the village, down there on the leafy southeastern fringe of London. Mark and Ryan were on the job, finishing up and I needed to head down myself to undertake some final checks. I asked Clare to find out how close the lads were to completion and instructed her to prepare the paperwork. She confirmed that they'd be done by the afternoon. She then promptly set up a meeting at the house with Mr Nestor, so that I could run some tests and hand over the system.

I felt as if I was functioning a little better than yesterday, though the sight of Darius working nearby reminded me of the whole TF thing. I figured that if the Birmingham project was already taken, then the least I could do was clear my desk and try to remain positive. With this in mind, I spent a productive hour-and-a-half attending to a range of relatively minor tasks.

At around 11:30am I popped into the coffee room. It was empty. As I was leaving, I bumped into the boss. I always feel a little nervous in his presence and I was particularly off-guard when he strode in with his cup. I greeted him politely as we passed each other. As I reached the door, he replied, in his regal tone "All set for Friday I hope...It's a big opportunity." I turned and mumbled a rather surprised "Yes", then seeing that he now had his back to me and was busy filling the kettle, I continued out of the coffee room.

This implied that the rumour about the hospital job might not be true after all. He sounded genuine enough and it seemed as if he was encouraging me to go for it. I was buoyed by the possibility that TF wasn't already lined up for promotion and that I, or should I say *we*, might therefore have a chance at landing the project.

I didn't mention it to Darius, nor Clare. Instead, I mulled over the prospect as I readied myself for the trip to Clive Nestor's. It struck me that I didn't have much of by way of a proposal. The presentations are on Friday, so I calculated that I had two days, as I would be busy all afternoon. There wasn't much time. I figured that if I really want the promotion, then I needed to put a solid plan together. I had to start as soon as possible.

With that in mind, I dug out the notes that Darius and I had put together, over beer and balti, which amounted to one sheet of curry-stained paper with a few scribbled points. I grabbed a new notepad and a pen from the stationery cupboard and headed out to Chislehurst.

Rather than driving through the midday traffic, I took the Tube, then an overground train out to the suburbs. The carriage was empty, so I sat at a table and worked on the proposal. I cast my mind back to our visit to the hospital and began thinking hard about its fire safety and emergency needs, as the train trundled through the scruffy inner boroughs just south of the river. The hospital's old system is way out of date, so the place needs a complete refit. We therefore have to start from scratch.

I opened the blank pad and wrote six headings on the first page–Detection, Warning, Suppression, Evacuation, Training and Monitoring. I then transferred our initial notes into these sections and started adding to them. It felt good to have made a start.

By the time the train had entered the endless suburban sprawl of semi-detached 1930's housing, that dominates much of southeast London, I'd already filled one side with notes. So I tore it out and gave each section its own separate sheet. The proposal was going to be bigger than I'd expected. If I want to get ahead of Twatface and his bolshie bullshit offensive, then I have to come up with something special–a bespoke, turn-key system that is comprehensive, yet affordable, and likely to last past the next tranches of safety legislation on the horizon.

I decided to produce a document that I can hand in to the boss in advance of the Friday meeting. I can then expand on it during my presentation. I want to show initiative and let him see that I really want the job. I caught a taxi from Chislehurst station to the Nestor's with the idea ringing in my mind.

Clive Nestor is in finance. I'm not sure how he makes his money exactly–banking, insurance, re-insurance, investment, hedge funds? But from the size of his house and the number of cars parked on his drive, he does pretty damn well for himself. I can't tell how old he is either, perhaps 45? He could be younger, but he always dresses in a suit, which can accentuate a person's age. His wife Natasha is eastern European, from one of the former Russian states. She comes across as rather cold and emotionless, but has an attractive face and a superb figure.

The Nestors have been a source of interest, speculation and envy during the month or so that we've been working for them. Mark and Ryan have been on site most the time and have fed us with information on the daily goings-on of this well-heeled household. It's mostly unimportant stuff, but Clare, in particular, laps it up, like they're the subject of some reality TV show.

Natasha Nestor is a certified woman of leisure. According to the lads, her daily routine consists of dropping their spoilt daughter 'Cupcake' to private school, in her gas-guzzling cream 4x4, then spending the rest of the day entertaining her equally well-to-do female friends at the house, or going on shopping trips and returning with copious bags of high-end merchandise. Rumour has it that she was a model before she had a kid. Like many other eastern Europeans, her body was left unaffected by the process. Mark and Ryan claim that she sometimes swims in their private indoor pool before lunch, then swans around the kitchen in her bathing suit.

I spotted Natasha's monstrous luxury car with its 'NN1' number plate as the taxi passed through the Nestor's electric gates and up their gravel drive. Clive's sports car was there too, parked alongside our grubby, white company van.

The job was indeed finished. Ryan was sweeping up multi-coloured wire cuttings from the floor of the fitness room and Mark was carrying tools and drums of cables through the house and into the van.

I began assessing the newly installed system, working room by room through the house, checking the smoke alarms, heat sensors, call points, emergency lighting, the alarm box, the escape routes and the water mist system. The latter was a point of contention with the Nestors. I advised them that domestic sprinklers are the way forward, as they increase escape time in the event of a fire and minimise property damage. But Natasha didn't like the look of the aspirators on the ceiling and moaned about them repeatedly. Mr Nestor was worried about the risk of water damage, but that's just a myth.

The system check lasted about an hour and took me through the entirety of the Nestor's palatial abode. Natasha emerged from the master bedroom in time for me to give it a look over. She was done up and looking fabulous. Given the time of day, she must have been off to pick up Cupcake from school. She walked past me without saying hello.

Clive Nestor was working on the computer in his wood-panelled study. I stood in the open doorway and knocked. He carried on tapping away for a minute or so, as if he was composing an email, before turning and giving me his attention.

I gave him a tour of the system, pointing out the full range of features that we'd installed, and instructing him on the use of them. He nodded and replied "Yeah. Yeah...OK. Yep" as I spoke, as if I was explaining something trivial. His phone rang as I was taking him through the operation of the main control box. He picked it up while I was in mid-sentence and wandered off to one side to take what appeared to be business call...I was clearly taking up his precious time, so I curtailed my introduction somewhat, then got him to sign the document that Clare had prepared. It stated that we were now handing over the system and that we'd be back to inspect it in six months. With that, I gave him the keys, shook his hand and left the house.

The lads were sitting in the van with the radio on. I got in beside them and we headed back to base.

Leaving the Nestor's mansion and passing by the gates of the similarly-proportioned properties along the same road, I reflected on my rather lowly position in the Nation's social hierarchy. I might be Applications Team Leader, in charge of a skilled group of technicians who'd just installed a complex fire safety system that may one day save lives, but to Clive and Natasha Nestor I'm just a relatively insignificant white-collar worker. Clive's attitude at the hand-over had said it all. He hadn't commented on the workmanship, which is of a very high standard, or even offered a 'thank you'. Instead he'd just wanted to sign the papers and get us out of his hair, and off his property. Our fascination with his upper-sclass life and the antics of his pampered, exotic wife suddenly seemed rather trivial. Clare will probably be talking about the Nestors for weeks to come, yet to them we're just another band of tradespeople, dealing with their extravagant needs.

Why is that I don't live in a mansion, or drive a £100,000 sports car? How come I'm not married to an Russian ex-model? Nestor can't be much older than me, so why am I so less successful than he is? Was he born into money, or did he just get lucky? He sounds privately educated, so he's probably got rich parents. If he went to public school then he could have used his old boys' network to get where he is...But he might also have worked very hard and had the determination to succeed in life. I guess that privilege and connections can only get you so far.

I certainly wasn't born with a silver spoon in my mouth. My parents aren't rich, nor well educated. I went to a shit comprehensive school, in which my classmates had no aspirations other than to do as little work as possible. In the light of this, getting into university was a great achievement. But I didn't exactly take advantage of the opportunity, graduating with only a third-class degree, then lazing about in London for several years afterwards. I did finally pull my finger out and get a half decent job, but it's taken me years to progress in any way.

Twatface has got the right idea. Despite being a total fucking tosser, he's not exactly waiting around to see what life brings his way. He's out to succeed. He probably uses me as benchmark of where he *doesn't* want to be at aged 40.

The rush hour traffic was awful. I should've just caught the train back and worked on my document. We arrived at the office around 5:40pm, so by the time I'd collected my things, closed down my computer and headed to the station, I'd already missed a couple of trains. I texted Fiona to let her know that I'd be on the next one.

As I emerged from the Underground, I spotted someone familiar in the distance–'Scarlet'. Though she was a fair few meters ahead of me and facing the other way, it was definitely her; I could spot her from a mile off. She was also heading for the train. As she neared the station and waited at a crossing, the gap between us narrowed.

Despite the tepid weather, she was wearing a rather short skirt. Her skinny, bare legs were suntanned, as if she'd just returned from holiday. This might explain why I've not seen her of late. As I followed a short distance behind her, onto the station concourse, I wondered how far her tan went up her sexy legs. Had she been on a European city break, wearing a mini-skirt or a little pair of shorts, or had she been sunning herself on a beach somewhere in the Med?

I ended up following Scarlet into the station, through the ticket barriers and onto the waiting train. Then realising that I was more or less stalking her, I stopped and sat down at an available seat. Unaware of my presence, she grabbed a free space across the aisle, facing in my direction.

I've only ever seen her on the platform in the morning and from a fair distance; it appears that she gets a later train home from whatever she does in London on a Tuesday. Now there she was, a couple of meters away, innocently gazing out of the window. What a sight! Her straight dark hair was neatly tied up and she had a healthy glow in her cheeks. She was wearing a cropped leather jacket, a white blouse, a short grey skirt and a pair of open-toed shoes. She really is a beauty! Though she looks younger up close.

We briefly exchanged glances as the train pulled away. I then got out my notes and attempted to work on the proposal. But I couldn't concentrate with Scarlet sitting in front of me. I stared blankly at the paper and occasionally looked up at her, trying not to make it too obvious. She was fiddling with her phone and looking out of the window, so I had plenty of opportunities to examine her in detail.

My eyes were drawn to the hem of her short skirt and her scrawny, bronzed appendages emerging from it. It gradually lifted up as she shifted in her seat, revealing her inner thigh and the briefest flash of her underwear, before she pulled it back down again. This got me very aroused. Her holiday tan reached right up her luscious legs, as far I could see. She'd definitely been on a beach. I pictured her sunbathing in a bikini. She had to look amazing.

By the time the train drew into the station, I had a full-on erection, which I was hiding beneath my notepad. Scarlet got up and headed for the door. I watched her, while waiting for my stiffy to subside, then got up and walked towards the exit myself. I stood close by her in a group of passengers as we waited for the train to come to a standstill. I caught her eye again and smiled, though rather nervously. She smiled back then looked away. It gave me butterflies.

The door slid open and we disembarked. I walked behind Scarlet as the crowd of passengers made its way out of the station. I watched her petite ass and the way her skirt brushed against it as she walked. There was no visible panty line, which meant that she was wearing a G-string. I pictured her in it, then imagined myself gently slipping her knickers down from behind and turning her around to reveal her pussy. God knows how amazing she is down there? Surely the stuff of dreams.

As I fantasised about disrobing Scarlet, we exited the station. A young lad on a moped with L-plates was waiting by the curb. He beeped his horn and waved at Scarlet. She ran up to him and they embraced. She then hopped on the back of his feeble-looking machine, donned a crash helmet and they rode off in a cloud of two-stroke fumes...

It immediately sunk in that luscious Scarlet, girl of my dreams and Tuesday morning eye candy extraordinaire, has to be a lot younger than I'd previously imagined. Her boyfriend, if that's who it was, can't be more than 18, so either she has a thing for zitty school-leavers or she's still only in her late teens herself. I'd assumed that she was in her early to mid 20's. I was a little shocked.

I mulled it over as I walked home from the station. Is this the type of women that I find most attractive–18, 19 year olds? That's less than half my age. Shouldn't my taste in women be a little more advanced as I approach my 40's? It's true that girls are more mature than boys at that age, but I'm old enough to be her dad. What was I doing following her and trying to catch her eye? Did I think that I stand a chance with her? There's no way she can find me attractive. I probably came over very creepy, and rather desperate.

Why am I so obsessed with younger women? It's not that I find women of my age unattractive, but I'm definitely fascinated by girls in their' 20's...and younger it seems.

It might be a hangover from my first girlfriend, Sue. I went out with her for a year, when I was in sixth-form and she was 16, and still at school. She was a real stunner. Unfortunately, she dumped me when I went to university. I was heartbroken for years. It might explain my obsession with Scarlet.

Internet porn is also surely to blame. Most of the websites feature girls of that age, or younger. Like Scarlet and Sue, their bodies are flawless, with tight, smooth skin, firm breasts and peachy bums. They've also got fresh innocent faces. Once women have started to decline from this ideal state, they become less photogenic and less attractive to us men, from a purely physical point of view. I guess it's a fact of life. But it still bothers me.

Will I still find 18-20 year olds irresistible when I'm 50? Suzy will be 16 by then and well on her way to becoming a woman herself. That would be very wrong! How can I ensure that this doesn't happen—that I don't end up fancying Suzy's school friends? It's going to be difficult as I get older and the average female of my equivalent age degenerates even further from the scrawny sex objects that I lust over on the Web. I definitely need to do something about it soon if I'm turning 40 in less than a week. But how?

Maybe I could make a start by viewing less porn? I could also pay more attention to Fiona. Her body doesn't come close to Scarlet's. How can it? She's got to be twice her age, and she's had two kids. Perhaps I need to stop judging her on these terms?

Suzy and Michael were in bed when I got home. I went straight up to see them. They've got their own rooms now, decorated pink and blue, and filled with gender-specific toys. Suzy is a little messy and always leaves things on the floor, which I often trip over when I go in to see her at night. She was just nodding off to sleep as I kissed her softly on the head.

When Fiona first got pregnant, I was convinced that we'd have a boy. We chose not to find out the sex of the baby until it popped out, so when Suzy arrived I was at first rather shocked. But as soon as I held her, felt her soft skin, smelled her and heard her gentle breathing, I immediately got over my initial disappointment. Though she is now six, she still has a baby-like quality, especially when she's sleeping.

Michael was fast asleep in his super-tidy room. He and Suzy couldn't be more different. Still, they get along pretty well. Not like my sister Margaret and I. I kissed his head and ruffled his hair. He's a good lad.

I got a son eventually. Though I was so converted to girls by the time Michael arrived that again, it took some getting used to. We found out the sex of our second in advance, so I was mentally prepared. Still, handling a baby boy wasn't the same, and I treated him differently from day one. I've always resented my father's favouritism towards Margaret and his rougher, hands-off approach to me. But since Michael came along, I've begun to understand it a bit.

Fiona was in the kitchen, preparing dinner. We'd hardly spoken since our argument on Sunday night, but things seemed to have cooled off a bit. We were both more pleasant and respectful to one another. She cooked chicken and chips and we shared the details of our respective days. I told her about yesterday's rumour at work and what my boss had said today. I mentioned the Nestor's job, but I didn't go into much detail. Fiona doesn't care much for gossip. Nor does she find rich or famous people particularly interesting.

Her day had been busy, particularly in the afternoon. She's been teaching German from home since we moved out of London. We were never going to afford two train fares as well as childcare, so she quit her office job and started advertising for language tuition, in shops and the local paper. She's slowly built up her business from there. Her students range from school kids needing extra lessons, to retired individuals who are off on holiday, or just interested in learning a language. Fiona studied French and German at university.

I washed up the dishes after dinner, which is the deal as I'm such a bad cook. Fiona was on the computer when I'd finished, so I watched an hour or so of TV and unwound. She joined me this time. We watched a documentary about the 1970's. We're both children of the 70's. It was an interesting program. The world was so different when we were growing up. It really showed our age. I worked out that Scarlet could have been born in the mid 90's. Fiona and I were already at uni by then.

Despite trying hard to rid my head of the image of Scarlet's sexy legs and ass, I was still very horny. As Fiona was in a better mood than yesterday, I tried my luck once we were in bed. I cautiously touched her breast in order to test the water. She immediately brushed my hand away, then after a pause asked me "Do you really think I'm going to have sex with you after yesterday?" I didn't reply. It clearly wasn't going to happen, so there was no sense in arguing.

We haven't done it for nearly six weeks. I remember the date of our last night of passion because it was Fiona's birthday. Prior to that we'd not had sex for a while either. She's surely due her period soon, which knocks off almost a week, so if we don't screw in the next few days, then it might be two months between shags. It's never been that long before. Making love has definitely become a much less frequent occurrence in recent years, especially since the birth of Michael, and I sense a problem developing. The problem isn't me. I'm always up for it. But if she keeps on rebuking me then I'll stop making a move on her, for fear of rejection and embarrassment. Then we might cease all together. It's happened to friends of ours

Fiona fell asleep pretty quickly, as she always does. I lay there, annoyed and sexually frustrated, until I couldn't take it anymore. So I went downstairs with the intention of relieving myself.

I've really gone off wanking of late. I still do it a lot, but it's just not a substitute for sex. It's great as a supplement, but when I'm not getting any of the proper stuff, it simply doesn't do the trick. I can wank on cue at any time of the day and in any place—the bogs, the shower, in a quiet corner, up a tree perhaps. I can just thrash out one after another, 'till my cock is red and stumpy, my arm hurts and there's no spunk left in my sack. But one hundred routine, run-of-the mill skanky wanks don't come close to a good deep fuck.

Remembering my decision to cut down on porn, I stayed off the computer and went into the lounge instead. I sat on the sofa in the dark and put my hands down my boxer shorts.

I tried to think of something that would get me aroused other than Scarlet or another nubile, naked fräulein of the type that I sometimes look at on the Web. Not much sprang to mind. I thought about Fiona, but I couldn't get stiff. I then imagined sleeping with a few of my friends' wives, who are Fiona's age or thereabouts. The thought of screwing one of them in particular did the trick. I'd certainly shag her—she's quite hot—but it was mostly the fantasy of being with another woman that got me hard.

I pulled myself off in the darkened room, trying to keep an appropriate image in my mind. It was a lot less arousing than sitting in front of the computer with a carefully selected porno shot to stimulate me. I struggled to maintain an erection.

Out of the corner of my eye, I noticed that the cat was also in the lounge. She was sitting there with one limb thrust vertically in the air and her head between her legs, cleaning her arse.

My cock went soft immediately.

Unable to relieve myself, I went back upstairs to bed. I still couldn't sleep. My mind was full of negative thoughts–about myself; about my life; about becoming 40. I went through a series of 'Yes' or 'No' questions in my mind: Am I happy? Am I satisfied? Am I having fun? Is this where I want to be at this point in my life? The answer to each question seemed to be a resounding 'No'. It was very depressing.

There was a time when I was positive about the future and excited by the here and now. These days I mostly look backwards in a nostalgic way to better times, wishing that those days would return. I used to use the past as a reference for how much better I was feeling at the present, rather than the other way around.

Perhaps I only remember the good times? I've certainly experienced many low points between the brief periods of immense joy. I used to think that good times always follow bad, and the sunny bits are so bright because of the extreme darkness that comes before them. But if this is true then why is it that life has felt so gloomy and tedious for such a long time? Where is the yang to go with all the yin I've been feeling? Did I overdose on joy to the point where I cannot feel it anymore? Or does it just dry up as one gets older?

I feel as if I'm trapped in a vicious cycle, endlessly repeating itself. Get up knackered; go to work; struggle to get through the day; make my way home, even more shattered; tuck the kids into bed, if I'm lucky; wash up after dinner; bicker with Fiona; go to bed worried about it all, then wake up early again, feeling unrefreshed and less able to cope with the next round of torture and drudgery than the day before.

Where is my escape from all this? Or is it simply my lot in life? Is it just the treadmill that I have to turn. How do I get off? How to I stop it from spinning and find time to gather myself? I wish I knew.

The second hand of the clock on our bedroom wall sounded incredibly loud as lay there reflecting in this depressing manner. It also appeared to be ticking faster than normal. I imagined that it signified my life, racing away at an ever-increasing rate into middle age.

My heart too was beating rapidly. I felt an indigestion attack coming on. I went to the bathroom to get a tablet. I also took two sleeping pills.

It took at least another hour for them to work.

Wednesday
39 YEARS, 361 DAYS

I was particularly knackered this morning on account of the pills I took last night. They got me off to sleep eventually, but I had a stormy night with intense, meaningless dreams, so I woke up really tired.

Luckily the weather has perked up a bit; it felt warmer and there were only scattered clouds in the sky, as I headed to the station. The weather really affects my mood these days. I get so depressed in winter when the days are short and the sky is grey for days on end. But when the sun is shining and the sky is blue, it lifts my spirit and makes my daily routine a whole lot more tolerable.

It was still not particularly sunny, but the forecast is better for the end of the week. They're even suggesting that it could be quite hot. We'll have to see about that. Back in June the weathermen were predicting the best summer in years, but it didn't materialise. We need at least a few more good days or the winter will be unbearable. I can't remember the last time I sunbathed. We couldn't afford a holiday this year.

A guy standing near me on the train was speaking to his loved one between the various bridges and tunnels. Their conversation sounded so pleasant. He had to be in his mid 30's, so unless he was having an affair, he clearly thought a lot of his partner, and she of him. He signed off in a beautifully upbeat manner and retained a smile on his face for a while after the call. It was sweet.

It reminded me of those early years with Fiona, when we were first in love. Oh to feel that again–the rush of new love...or even the warm flickering of a diminished yet eternal flame. We have our moments, but compared to the genuine sincerity that was audible in the guy's tone, we're like two old souls that have grown too familiar with each other, and tired of one another's company.

I met Fiona at university in Leicester, when I was in my second year and she was a fresher. I was manning the table for 'Juggling Society' at the freshers' fair, when a gaggle of fresh-faced first-year girls turned up. They were all from the same student hall of residence and had been at college for barely a week. I somehow convinced them that juggling was the thing to do, despite having only been introduced to it a few months earlier by my flat mate, and they parted with £2 before disappearing back into the throng of excited students.

I didn't remember Fiona from that encounter. A taller dark-haired friend of her's stuck in my mind instead. But at the inaugural juggling club meet, which was basically a bunch of people throwing stuff around the refectory, I found myself tutoring her and one of the other girls on how to keep three balls in the air—a feat that I'd only recently learnt myself.

Fiona had wide sparkling eyes and wavy strawberry-blonde hair. She's exactly the same height as me, but when I think back to that first encounter, I see her looking up at me—literally, as well as for my superior juggling skills. The first year of university was such a crucial period for me in a lot ways; I experienced many things for the first time. After three terms of independent life, I felt like a real man-about-town, though in reality I was just a naive 19 year-old student layabout. Fiona had just moved up from rural Surrey and the comfort of her parents' home, so I guess I must have come over as much older and more experienced.

After a few juggling club meets, Fiona approached me at the students' union, on a Friday night. I worked behind the bar at that point. She appeared out of the mass of stupefied punters, smiling at me. I had a break five minutes later, so I agreed to meet her. I brought a complimentary half-pint of snake-bite-and-black for her and we chatted by the crowded stairwell that linked the various shabby bars and dance-floors of the union. Out of the blue, she kissed me on the lips. That's how it started.

I was surprised at how forward Fiona had been. She wasn't quite the innocent girl that I'd assumed. It seemed that she'd liked me straight away, so she just went after me. I was still mourning the loss of Sue and I hadn't moved on; no one compared to her as far I was concerned. Still, I didn't resist Fiona's advances and after a couple of weeks we appeared to be 'going out'. The sex was regular and of a good standard, as far as I could tell. More importantly though, she gave me my space when I needed it, so I could hang out with my college mates and pursue my other interests, which over the course of the second year switched from juggling and beer to dance music and weed.

I remember our first year as boyfriend and girlfriend as a warm, rosy time. We had few cares or worries. Life just flowed naturally and we had a lot of fun together. Oh what I'd give to have those days back!

I was still sexually frustrated after last night. I found myself glancing at the glossy calling cards pinned up in the telephone boxes along the street, between the Tube station and my work. The ladies on the flyers are surely not the prostitutes themselves. There's a 'sauna' nearby. I walk past it every day. It's just a metal door with frosted glass, between a shop and some sort of red brick apartment block. I've never seen anyone go in or out of it. I've always suspected that it's a knocking shop. I often wonder what it's like in there—a mysterious seedy world just off the street.

Mates of mine have shagged prostitutes, on a stag weekend in Prague some years ago. We ended up in a strip joint and some of the lads went upstairs with a girl. I was very tempted, but I managed to resist. Some of the ladies were very tasty. Inner-city London prozzies have got to be pretty rough in comparison.

With Mark and Ryan back at the office, I took the opportunity to quiz everyone on the Birmingham hospital job. I took them for coffee, down in the plaza. They'd already gathered from the chatter in the office that the TF rumour was bullshit.

The guys offered some useful suggestions, particularly Clare, which I added to my notes. Darius and Ryan made jokes in a brummie accent. To them it's just another job I guess. Mark says he wouldn't mind the nights up in Birmingham, to get away from 'the missus' and go drinking.

At lunch I returned to the same café with a laptop, to work on the document. I grabbed a cozy spot in the corner and typed away while drinking coffee and eating a panini. I transferred my notes into a blank file. The hospital has certain obvious needs that can be neatly categorised within the six headings in my notepad. What I needed however, was an overall theme; a standout philosophy that would catch the attention of the boss.

Realising that I was running out of time to get the document ready for tomorrow, I decided to pull out all stops...I called Fiona from the café and told her that I'd be working late, and that I'd grab something to eat up in London. I figured that if she wasn't going to let me screw her any time soon, then there was no need for me to rush home. I could focus my pent up energy on the document instead. For once I sounded determined. She must have sensed it, as she said that I should take as much time as I needed.

I received a text in the afternoon from my old friend Jason. He's a DJ. We haven't seen each other for a few years. He recently turned 40 himself and celebrated at a trendy nightclub. I didn't attend, as we couldn't get a babysitter–though I didn't really fancy it anyway. He enquired what I'm doing on Sunday. I've no plans yet for my birthday. He then invited me out for drinks in London tomorrow. I said that I'd let him know. I was quite focused on the proposal and I didn't want to think about anything else.

I stayed late at work, as planned. I've only done so a handful of times before. I popped out to get some fish and chips and a coke, which I spread on my desk and ate while I worked. The last person left at 6:30pm, then it was just me, alone in the open-plan office, typing away.

With nothing to distract me except the sound of London down below, my brain suddenly came alive. I channelled the energy that had built up in me during the afternoon into the document. It felt strangely enjoyable to be working after hours in my own time.

I still needed a concept to hang the proposal and my presentation on, so I pulled up the hospital's website and searched for inspiration. It's a big place with several separate buildings. It struck me why the boss needs a single team working on the job, full time, and why he wants us to compete against each other for it. It's going to be a serious undertaking, so we need the best group to take charge. Considering the scale of the project, I suddenly doubted whether I'm up to it.

I re-read what I'd written. It sounded surprisingly good; it sounded professional. Some of it was pretty bullshitty and generic, but there was some slick stuff in the document. It's perhaps what I need to aim for–to be more business-like and perhaps a little bit cocky...to be a bit more like Twatface? I also need a challenge to kick me up the arse, or others in the firm will pass me by. There's no reason why I can't manage the project. I just need to make sure that I get assigned to it in the first place. That'll hopefully give me the confidence boost to see it through.

As I browsed the website a little more it occurred to me that we and the hospital have similar goals. We're both in the business of protecting people. We detect risks and alert the public to them. We deal with the risks as they progress and above all, we try to mitigate and minimise damage and loss. It was a Eureka! moment.

Realising that our objectives and those of the hospital align with one another, I decided to reorganise the document around this idea, and turn it into the theme of my presentation. My original six headings slotted in quite well or ran through the proposal.

I spent about hour reworking the document. It was nearly dark outside by the time I'd finished. I checked my watch. It was 8:30pm. I was working with an exhilarating natural flow and determination–though some of my energy was down to the coke and coffee I'd been drinking–so I decided to also have a crack at the presentation, before I left the office.

I called Fiona again. She was watching TV. She'd already eaten and put the kids to bed. I informed her that I was going to be while longer. Once more, I felt an unusually determined tone in my voice. Again, she seemed to sense it too, as she immediately confirmed that it was OK for me to keep on working.

I briefly wondered whether Fiona might suspect that I was up to something, behind her back. It's certainly not normal for me to work so late. For all she knew I could've been having a secret rendezvous. If she suspected anything, it didn't show in her voice. I found the idea of making her jealous rather amusing.

The presentation took me another hour. I kept it simple, restricting each slide to one or two suitable images of the hospital and the types of installations that I propose they'll need. I accompanied these with a few bullet-points, which I can expand on. As it's unlikely that the boss will read the whole document before the meeting, I figured that I can recite from it and beef up my slides. It was another moment of clear thinking and quick decision-making.

By the time I'd locked up the office and set the alarm, around 9.30pm, I was brimming with energy and excitement. I took a printout of the document with me to read on the train home. It was still quite warm outside. I withdrew some cash in the plaza with the intention of buying some beers at the station for the journey home. In my haste, I accidentally pressed the wrong button and the machine dispensed me £100 rather than £10.

Taking my usual shortcut from to the Tube station I again passed by the 'sauna'. Light was shining through its nondescript frosted door and illuminating the otherwise dark street. It was the first time that I'd seen any sign of life coming from the place.

Seeing that the street was empty, I paused by the door. It suddenly seemed inviting. I stood for a second or two and considered going in. The thought sent a shiver down my spine. With London's workday population now gone home, I figured that I wasn't likely to be spotted by anyone that I knew. I looked around again...then I pushed the stiff metal-framed glass door and went inside...

I immediately found myself at the foot of some stairs, beside which was simple office counter, built into the wall. An Arab, perhaps in his 20's, was sat behind it. He looked at me blankly. There was no lobby nor reception area—just the counter and a set of steep stairs. I'd hoped to be able to look around a bit. Given that the entrance was sandwiched between two other buildings, it was obvious that the premises itself had to be upstairs. I couldn't go any further without declaring what it was that I was after.

I must have looked rather startled. I was about to leave when I noticed a board on the wall, behind the counter. I quickly studied its contents: "Mon-Thurs, Sun–£21, Fri-Sat–£30, Couples–£30/40, Massage–£25." The place did indeed appear to be a sauna. I didn't exactly fancy a soak in a jacuzzi or therapeutic rub. I'd come in because I expected that they offered personal services. The last item at the bottom of the board was "Private Massage" with no price.

I looked at the chap again, who was still staring at me. Realising that I ought to either choose an activity or leave the building, I blurted out "Private Massage please." He abruptly replied "Eighty pounds." I paused again, once more surprised. At eighty pounds a private massage had to be what I'd expected. I was right, it was a knocking shop.

Having satisfied my curiosity, I wasn't sure what to do next. I considered leaving, but what was I going to say to excuse myself–that I'd changed my mind or that it was too expensive? I felt a little embarrassed. Not wanting to look like an idiot, or even worse, like a desperate guy who'd never been with a prostitute before and was having second thoughts, I reached for my wallet and drew out the £100 that I'd accidentally dispensed from the cash machine a short while ago.

The guy took £80 off me. He gave me a white towel from under the counter, then pointed at the stairs and said "Room 2...Showers on left."

I took the towel and ascended the stairs. I felt a huge rush of nerves and excitement as I realised what I'd just done.

The top of the narrow, poorly lit staircase opened into altogether more pleasant and brighter part of the establishment. A corridor led into the building, with several doors coming of it. The first door on the left swung open and a man appeared. He was bare-chested and wearing one of the white towels. He strolled off down the corridor, past a large potted palm and into another part of the building.

I entered the changing rooms and got undressed. I placed my belongings in one of the lockers and had a quick shower. I was still quite nervous and somewhat in disbelief at what I was doing. Fiona might now be in bed, and there I was, in a sauna in a seedy part of central London, about to receive a 'massage' from a prostitute. It shocked and excited me in equal measures. If she found out then it would be the end of us for sure. But if she didn't then it might be incredibly titillating and devious. It could be what I needed to satisfy my severe sexual frustration. On the other hand it might be awful, embarrassing and degrading, especially if the prostitute was hideous.

I had no idea of what awaited me inside Room 2 and what the implications of going in there might be. But I'd now gone too far to turn back. I'd parted with the money and I was standing in a towel with time running out for me to get my train home. If this was something that I wanted to try, just the once, and something that I needed to do before Sunday, then this was the moment.

I studied myself in the changing room mirror, conscious that I was about get naked with a woman that I'd never met. I re-arranged my hair to cover the bits where it's receding and pulled in my stomach. I wanted to make a good impression; I didn't want to come over as an frustrated, under-sexed, married man. I took off my wedding ring and placed it in the locker, in my trouser pocket...I suddenly felt single. It was exciting.

I left the changing rooms and headed for Room 2. It was just along the corridor. I knocked and heard a muffled "Come in." I turned the handle and entered.

The room was small and rather bare, but like the rest of the sauna, it looked and smelt clean.

There was a double bed covered with a white sheet, a bedside table and a small lamp. In the corner, a woman was standing at a wash-basin, with her back to me. She had wavy, dyed, red hair, a heavily tattooed back and a green sarong tied around her waist. "Jost be a minute" she announced in strong Irish accent.

I stood just inside the door, near the foot of the bed, until she'd finished and turned round. She had a pretty face and small breasts. She smiled, then untied her sarong and draped it over the lamp, immediately changing the mood of the room. She placed a condom on the bedside table and climbed onto the bed, naked.

She lay on her back resting on her elbows and looking towards me. Realising that she was now ready, I undid my towel and approached the bed. I'd not been unclothed in front of another woman for many years, save for once at the doctors. I was a little shy, but at the same time rather excited. I looked at my cock. It was starting to get hard.

The prostitute was more attractive than I'd expected. She had to be in her mid 20's. She had a pleasant face, a pretty slim body, nice tits and a shaved pussy. It was completely bare down there— nothing was left to the imagination.

I reached for the condom and began to put it on. It had been ages since I'd last worn one of those horrid things—nearly two decades. They still have the same slimy texture and sickly smell. I fumbled to stretch it over my erect penis, while she watched. Seeing that I had it on, she opened her legs in anticipation.

This was it! This was the moment that I redeemed the casual sex that I'd just payed for. There was no need for courtship nor foreplay; no suspense nor doubt as to whether I was going to score. She simply lay there in front of me, with a rather blank expression on her face, naked and ready to go. All that was left to do was for me to indulge myself.

I got onto the bed and manoeuvred myself over her. I lowered myself down onto her naked body, letting my cock press against her groin. She looked me in the eye and smiled as our bodies came into contact.

After many years of fantasising about sleeping with another woman, I was about to find out what it's like. Her bare skin felt warm and soft beneath me. I could smell her perfume and feel her curly hair brush against my arm. It was exhilarating.

I reached down and grabbed my cock, ready to direct it into position and start screwing her...But something stopped me. It somehow didn't feel right; something was amiss. I paused for a moment, with my chest suspended above her breasts, unsure of what to do. I was confused.

Sensing that there was a problem, she asked me "Yer OK?" I looked back at her not knowing what to say. "First time?" she continued. I looked away.

I realised that I couldn't do it. It wasn't what I wanted. It was definitely a very sexual experience and she was pretty fuckable, but it felt too unfamiliar; her touch, her smell, her voice–they didn't seem right. It wasn't what I'm used to…She wasn't Fiona. I didn't like it.

I apologised and got off her. She didn't look too happy.

I felt very embarrassed. I wanted to get up and leave, but it would've seemed rather rude. It also struck me that I'd just wasted £80 that I couldn't really afford.

I didn't know what to do or say next. We both looked at each other for a moment, in silence, until I blurted out "What's your name?" She seemed rather confused by my randomness, but after a brief pause, she replied "Dey call me Lucky."

We had a friendly chat, sitting there on the bed, naked, with my cock now limp. We didn't talk about what had just happened.

She was from Tipperary. She'd come over to London a year ago to find work and experience a new place. She'd worked in a pub, then as a stripper before starting at the sauna. She spoke very openly about her line of work, as if she wasn't ashamed. I also got the impression that she'd not been forced into it.

Lucky struck me as a very pleasant and rather honest person. In spite of her many tattoos, which gave her a somewhat edgy look, she clearly took pride in her appearance. Her bright red hair was carefully permed and she had a distinctly floral smell to her. She was far from the horrific, drug-addicted hooker that I'd expected to be waiting for me. She also seemed intelligent and sharp.

I enjoyed chatting to her. It helped me relax. She also seemed to appreciate it. We didn't speak about what had just happened.

Realising that I'd been in the room with Lucky for a while, I apologised to her again and thanked her for her company.

I grabbed my towel, left the room and went to get changed. Checking my watch, I saw that it was nearly 11:00pm. I needed to move in order to make the last train. I quickly dressed, left the building and continued my journey through night-time London, to the Tube, then across town to the train station.

I nervously texted Fiona once I was on the train to let her know that I was on my way back. I didn't get a reply, so I gathered that she'd gone to bed.

The train was rather empty. I sat there thinking about what I'd just done, still exhilarated, but also a little shocked. I was struck by how easy it is to walk in off the street and have sex with a stranger. If I'm ever feeling desperate again and Fiona isn't responding to my manly urges, then I can go back in, ask for Lucky and get a shag. It's as simple as that–a cash transaction for a basic service, that for many men is hard to come by.

Despite this, I was a little put off by the prospect of satisfying my urges in this way. Being with a stranger was just *too* different, after so many years with the same woman. I've gotten so used to Fiona in this time that it felt wrong.

I'd certainly satisfied my curiosity. But was this what I wanted; what I needed? It was far too easy to be unfaithful. Surely something so significant as cheating warrants a little more forethought?..I've done it only the once before and I vowed never to do it again. For that reason I was kicking myself.

My 'affair', as Fiona used to call it, happened a long time ago. I was very young and we were only just starting out as a couple. After our pleasant first year together at university, Fiona spent a year abroad in Germany as part of her language degree, while I completed my third and final year of study. We'd grown quite close by then, and Fiona in particular was very fond of me. We didn't discuss what would happen when she left for her trip, instead we just carried on seeing each other. I was too wrapped up with my mates and going out to give it much thought, until Fiona actually left and I returned to university alone.

I enjoyed my own space at first, but I eventually missed the regular sex and to some extent, her company. Fiona, being emotionally more mature than I was at the time, really missed me. We spoke regularly from a telephone box on campus and she sent many letters, declaring her love for me.

One night, while I was out with my pals at the students' union, I ended up chatting with Fiona's friend Sheri. She was the tall, dark-haired hottie that I'd noticed at the freshers' fair the year before. She was very flirty and enquired about Fiona and I.

A few weeks later at a nightclub in Leicester city-centre, I bumped into her again and she hit on me. None of Fiona's other friends ventured into the clubs in town, so there was little chance that anyone would see us. I still fancied Sheri rotten, so I snogged her. Before I knew it, we'd slept together, back at mine, and I'd done the dirty on Fiona.

Sheri had a boyfriend at uni, but it was widely known that he was still seeing a girl from his hometown. Looking back, it's clear that she was just using me to get back at him. But at the time, I was happy to be getting some casual sex to fill the gap left by Fiona.

Sheri and I screwed on and off for most of the first term, tying to keep it a secret. Fiona called and wrote letters as normal and it seemed that she was unaware of what was going on behind her back.

It wasn't long until she found out though. She returned for Xmas and came up to Leicester, before the end of term. After a day or two, someone must have told her. She challenged me and I had no choice but to own up. She was terribly upset. We headed off to our respective parents for Xmas with our fledgling relationship on the rocks.

I didn't see Fiona before she went back out to Germany in the new-year. I assumed that it was more or less over between us. But just to make sure, I wrote her a long break-up letter. I was embarrassed about the affair and I wanted to dump her before she officially dropped me. It was a very cowardly and immature thing to do, but I felt that I could easily move on and get another girlfriend– perhaps Sheri, perhaps someone else.

Unfortunately, Sheri didn't want to know me after the drama with Fiona; she had a boyfriend anyway. Without her casual sex and attention, I slowly lost confidence in myself. The Leicester student community was a small world, so everyone knew about my infidelity. People either thought that I was an idiot, or a cheating bastard. By the summer term, some of my clubbing mates now had serious girlfriends and I still hadn't met anyone.

I eventually regretted being unfaithful to Fiona and I longed to have her back. My parents thought the world of her and they were naturally disappointed that we'd split up. They of course didn't know the whole story.

During a home visit, just before the exams, I opened up to them. They offered to pay my fare to Germany, so that I could try and get Fiona back. It was a nice gesture. In a rare moment of rational decision-making, I swallowed my pride and took them up on their offer.

I was meant to contact Fiona in advance of my mission to win her back. I informed my parents that I had done, but I was too embarrassed. I figured that I'd just turn up and whisk her off her feet. After a two-day coach trip, I turned up on her doorstep, looking and feeling rather rough. She was certainly surprised, but not however particularly happy to see me.

I spent three days at her student digs, sleeping on the sofa and feeling very stupid. It was clear that she'd not sat around crying since I'd dropped her. Instead, she'd really settled into life abroad, without the distraction of her unfaithful ex-boyfriend. She was speaking fluent German and she'd made many new friends. They looked at me with suspicion. It was also obvious that she'd slept with other guys, though she insisted that she was still single.

I'd expected Fiona to take me back straight away, but she made me sweat it out instead. On the last day of my stay I broke down and cried. I told her that I loved her and I apologised profusely. I promised that if she took me back then I'd never cheat on her again.

My desperate pleading worked...When she returned that summer, after my final exams, we were a couple again. She arrived back in time for my graduation ceremony. She sat with my parents in the audience. They were as pleased as pie!

My one and only experience of infidelity certainly put me off cheating. It's for this reason that I've not had another affair, nor gone with a prostitute, until now.

I tried to rationalise what I'd just done with Lucky. Yes, I'd gotten naked with her for 10 minutes or so, at the most. Yes, I'd felt my erect cock against her bare pussy. It was a sex act, for sure. But did it mean that I'd cheated? It wasn't proper sex; I'd not penetrated her. I'd also payed for the pleasure. Fiona has starved me of sex for so long, that I'd been forced to find pleasure elsewhere.

Based on these facts, I justified to myself that I'd not been unfaithful in the same way as my fling with Sheri...Of course Fiona might disagree if she ever finds out, but that's how I see it.

In an ideal world, I'd screw as many women as possible. I often fantasise about having sex with other women–people I know, women I see in the street, or even just an ideal imaginary female that fits my particular physical preferences. It's definitely been hard staying monogamous for nearly two decades, especially in recent years. But in reality, being unfaithful is probably too risky at this point in my life. It would be foolish to jeopardise our marriage and the stability of our family. I wouldn't want to throw all that away just for a quick adulterous shag.

It might also be less satisfying than I'd expected. I mean, how would I have felt if I'd unloaded into Lucky? What would be going through my mind moments after I've slept with one of Fiona's friends, or nailed young Scarlet in her parents house? Once the pleasure subsides, I'll probably be a little ashamed with myself. It would be a big come-down after a short, though perhaps very sweet, moment of excitement.

I've got to admit that Fiona has always trusted me since my fling with Sheri. I've rarely sensed any jealousy when it comes to other women. Perhaps she could see, on that last day in Germany, that I'd learnt my lesson?

That may have been the moment that the tables were turned on our relationship and Fiona gained the upper hand. I'd betrayed her and she'd given me a second chance. For that reason, I feel like I've always been in her debt. Though she said that she'd forgiven me, she still brought it up for several years afterwards, during arguments. It was her trump card that I could never match.

That episode could've been the start of our gradual slide from young, passionate lovers to middle-aged celibate hermits; it may have been the catalyst. Fiona used to look up to me, she used to dote over me and she used to give herself to me at any opportunity. Now she seems to resent me, she ignores my needs and she constantly withholds herself from me.

Perhaps what I need to get over my sexual frustration, instead of a causal fuck with a Lucky or an affair with Scarlet, is to rekindle the desire that Fiona felt for me in those early years? If she could just rediscover the man that she fell in love with at university, and the man that she took back after he betrayed her. She used to fancy me; she used to find me irresistible; she used to love having sex with me. I didn't need to ask, nor did I need to wonder whether she'd turn me down or not. I was in control, not her. How can I turn back the tables? How can I re-conquer her in the bedroom?

While I was going over this in my mind and thinking occasionally about Lucky's shaven pussy, I noticed the mark on my finger where my wedding ring normally sits. Ten years of wearing it has left a permanent impression in my skin. I reached into my trousers to retrieve the ring and put it back on. But it wasn't there...I frantically searched my pockets, then searched them again. I checked the floor of the train carriage and between the cushions of the seat, but I couldn't find it anywhere. My heart started pounding as I realised that it must have fallen out– perhaps at the sauna, perhaps on the Tube, or at the train station, or maybe in the street. Shit!!

I couldn't believe it. I'd lost my wedding ring somewhere in London. Fuck! Fuuck!! Fuuuck!!! What the hell was I going to do? How was I going to explain myself? What plausible excuse could I have for taking off my ring and losing it? I never take it off. There's no need to. The only two reasons for taking it off are if we got divorced, or if I was up to no good. Why the hell did I take it off in the first place? So that the prostitute might think I was single, and ask me out for a date? What a complete and utter idiot. I was really in the shit!

I considered getting off at the next stop and catching a train back up to London, if there was one. But it could take ages to retrace my steps and I'd need to catch a taxi home. How would I explain that to Fiona? What could I have possibly left in London that couldn't wait 'till the next day? If I'd lost my wallet then I could just cancel my credit cards over the phone. Anyway, if I did get off and trek back up, there was no guarantee that I'd find my ring. I'd no choice but to go home without it.

I calmed down a little and tried to think of an alternative plan. If I'd left the ring at the sauna then perhaps it'd be found and they'd hold onto it. It was a long shot. If I'd dropped it at the train station or on the Tube then it might also be handed in. I could ask in the morning. If I'd lost it somewhere on the street in London, then it was more or less gone and I would be well-and-truly buggered!

But what was I going to do when I got home? Hopefully Fiona would be asleep. In the morning I could try to avoid her and hide my left hand. I could slip out of the house and hope to god that I could find the ring up in London. I could pop into the station offices and call the Underground lost-and-found number. The sauna wasn't likely to be open at 8:30am on a Thursday morning, so I'd have to wait 'till lunch, or perhaps go there after work. That's if I hadn't yet recovered it elsewhere.

If the ring *was* lost then I needed another plan. I either had to come clean with Fiona or buy a replacement. Owning up had to be my last resort, as it would unleash a world of pain and sadness. I wondered whether I could get away with buying a new one. It's a pretty simple gold band, albeit with an inscription inside. Fiona might not notice. It was a feasible plan, but if I couldn't check at the sauna until the evening, then I might not have time to get hold of a new ring before returning home. I didn't want to have to hide my hand and avoid Fiona for two nights. That would far be too risky.

Walking home from the station, I remembered that there's a jewellers in the High Street. I could perhaps buy something there in the morning before I go to work. They might have a cheap-ish, gold-coloured ring. It needn't be real gold. I just have to fool Fiona until I can get hold of a more convincing replacement, complete with engraving.

I was feeling very nervous as I turned into our street. On approaching the house, I noticed that the lounge light was on. Fiona was still up. It was the last thing I needed!

I cautiously opened the font door, took off my shoes and tiptoed towards the lounge. I could hear the TV, so she was definitely still up. I nervously popped my head around the doorframe...

Fiona was curled up on the sofa. She was wearing what looked like one of my work shirts, and not much else. She smiled warmly, then got up and approached. She'd done her hair and she had make up on. She looked nice. I knew what this meant—she was finally horny and ready for sex. It caught me by surprise. I must have looked shocked. I was still trying to hide my hand behind the door.

We kissed, then headed straight upstairs to the bedroom. Fiona had lit some candles. I was glad of the atmospheric lighting. We lay on the bed. I undid the shirt, then got inside her. It was the second time in one night that I'd been naked with a woman—something that I'd never experienced before.

We made love. It felt great after such a long time, but I took ages to come. I was still thinking about the ring and trying to avoid Fiona touching my left hand. She grabbed it at one point, but luckily she didn't notice.

She looked up at me with genuine passion as I thrust back and forth into her, as if she'd been gagging for it as much as I had.

I watched her close her eyes and open her mouth as she started to come. I always like that moment—when she finally lets herself go. She wears an altogether friendlier and loveable face than the one that glares at me when she's angry. I genuinely despise looking at her sometimes—when we are both at each other's throats, arguing for some petty reason. But when she's letting me make love to her, I remember the night that we first did it in my tiny student room. When I'm inside her and she is coming, it never fails to turn me on.

As I watched Fiona orgasm, I temporarily forgot about the ring and I started to let myself go too. After a few more minutes of pumping I began to climax. It started as a small tingle in the pit of my stomach, then quickly spread through my body, increasing exponentially in an almighty crescendo of pleasure that finally blasted out of me, through my penis. It was catastrophic release of pressure, anxiety and semen that had built up over many weeks of hard work, stress, poor sleep and lack of sex—the early starts; the endless repeating slog of commuting into London and back home again; the responsibility at work; the boredom at work; the busy chore-filled weekends; the worries about money; the worries about my age; the worries about us. Everything seemed to be coming out of me in one almighty explosion. I could hardly breathe as came deep into Fiona. It was almost painful. I shouted "Fuuuuuuuck!", then collapsed on top of her.

It took me a minute or two to catch my breath. I slumped beside Fiona on the bed. I was exhausted and my arms and legs were numb. I let my left arm hang out of the bed, out of sight.

A blissful melancholic feeling came over me— a post-coital state of total relaxation. I love that brief halcyon afterglow, when all seems rosy and complete. It often puts me straight to sleep. Instead, I lay there, eyes half closed, staring at the ceiling, enjoying it. I'd not had such a powerful orgasm for a long time, nor had I felt so deeply satisfied in the minutes following. For a moment, all my cares and worries had melted away.

Fiona held my right hand and let out a sigh of pleasure herself. We'd finally made love. Why it'd taken so long wasn't exactly clear. Something had prevented her from succumbing to my advances. It might have been her; it could also have been me.; it was probably also due to a whole host of external factors. But at last it had happened.

The warmish weather earlier in the day had continued into the evening, so we lay there naked, side-by-side, on top of the bedclothes, in the candle-lit bedroom, chatting. With the air cleared between us, it was as sincere a conversation as we'd had in a while.

I told Fiona about the document and the enthusiasm that I'd felt at the office earlier in the evening. She sounded very pleased and encouraged me to hand it in. It wasn't just the money or the new kitchen, she explained, but also that she wants to see me progress at work and get over my boredom. I'm definitely bored at work. I'm bored of doing the same thing day-in day-out and not getting a pay rise. I bring my boredom and frustration home and Fiona surely feels it. Maybe my boredom bores her? Maybe it turns her off? She seemed happy that I'd at least temporarily found something that I was enthusiastic about, even if it meant that I'd needed to work late at the office.

I asked Fiona about her day, then about her work in general. Though it's going OK and she reckons that she's just about as busy as she can manage, what with looking also after the house and dropping and picking the kids up, she didn't sound terribly happy. She admitted to being a little bored of working from home. Though she's made a few friends in the village—mostly with other mothers on the school run—it's a very small place. She misses working in London and the daily buzz of a big city. As we spend most weekends at home, she rarely experiences a change of scenery. It's something that I take for granted I guess. I suggested that we should go up to London some weekend with the kids, or perhaps go out in town one evening–just the two of us, like old times. She liked the idea.

I mentioned that Jason has asked me out for a catch-up beer tomorrow after work. Fiona and I used to hang out with him when we moved up to London after university. We also went on holiday to Ibiza together. She encouraged me to go, even though it'll mean me coming home late again. She said it would be good for me. I'm still not sure if I can make it. I've got a lot to do tomorrow and I need to stay focussed for Friday.

We got onto the subject of Sunday and my birthday. I shared with Fiona some of my hang-ups about getting older and turning 40–about the years just disappearing, about the stress and boredom of daily life, about money, and about us arguing more and more and sleeping with each other less and less. It was good to get it off my chest.

It turns out that Fiona is as equally insecure about getting old as I am. She's also approaching the end of her 30's. She argued that it was harder for a woman; men can get away with the physical side-effects of ageing easier than women. She's worried about her body and about her looks. Like me, she also wonders where the years have gone. I've been so wrapped up in my own quadrophobia that it hadn't occurred to me that she might be suffering as well.

I asked Fiona if she still has the urge for another child. She doesn't. She said that if she'd gotten pregnant a couple of years ago, straight after Michael, then perhaps she'd have been pleased. But it's no longer something that she wants or needs. She reckons her child-bearing days are over.

I asked her what it is that she wants out of life at the moment. She isn't sure exactly, though she listed a few things. They're pretty much the same simple things that I want, like more free-time, more money, more fun and fewer responsibilities. She didn't mention more sex, which is high on my list of priorities, but I felt that we'd just made progress on that after a stupidly long gap. I know that I can definitely help the situation by believing in myself a bit more and giving her something to desire. Given Fiona's own insecurities, I also need to pay her more attention and make her feel attractive.

Though I was still feeling quite relaxed, I started to think once more about the ring as we got under the duvet and turned off the light. The jewellers might not open until 9:00am tomorrow, so I've no choice but to call in sick. If all goes well then I can make it into work sometime mid-morning.

Just before I dosed off I thought about the sauna and Lucky the prostitute, about my lost ring and about the sex I'd just had with Fiona. It had been a rather eventful evening to say the least.

Thursday
39 years, 362 days

My alarm went off at the usual time. I'd slept well. I immediately remembered last night and my missing wedding ring. I had a busy day ahead of me. I pretended that I was ill and asked Fiona if she could give the kids breakfast. She reluctantly agreed, leaving me to lay in for half-an-hour.

I almost never get a lie-in these days. We used to sleep 'till midday on a Saturday or Sunday, before the children arrived. There's no chance of that anymore. Just five or ten minutes extra kip is a treat. With the bed to myself, I spread out and had the most heavenly doze. It felt extremely indulgent.

Despite the potentially disastrous situation with the ring and the fact that I was going to be late for work, I felt pretty relaxed. Getting my oats last night was a great relief. It's funny how sex can improve your mood—releasing pressure and anxiety, and giving you a boost of energy.

I was woken again by Suzy. She'd finished her breakfast and come up to ask if I was OK. She got into bed with me and we had a quick cuddle. It was lovely.

I then had an idea. If I was going to pull a sickie, then it would be a good opportunity to take her to school. I sent her into her room to get dressed, while I called work. The receptionist wasn't in yet, so I left a message in a croaky voice. I'm rarely off sick, so I reckoned that one morning would be OK.

Fiona reappeared as I was showering. I informed her that I was feeling a little better. She was happy not to have to do the school run. She seemed in a good mood despite having to get up earlier than usual. Things felt better between us. She enquired whether I was going out with Jason. I'd forgotten about it. I took a change of clothes with me, in case I fancied it later.

I had to run the gauntlet with the ring, so I was very relieved when Suzy and I could leave the house. I walked her to school. I held her little hand and we chatted. We passed the park, so I let her have 10 minutes in the playground. She had the place to herself. I sat on a bench and watched her joyfully playing.

I can still imagine holding Suzy as a newborn baby, as if it was last year, not six years already. She was so small that she almost fitted in my palms. It's hard to believe, looking at her now. It's also strange to think that I was only 34 when she popped out. I wasn't the youngest dad that ever lived, but I'm surprised and also kind of proud that I coped with the responsibility.

Kids are such a good, or maybe bad, barometer of age. Watching them grow and develop really highlights the passage of time. They really underline how much older you've become. After a year or so, it's hard to remember life without them. You're so knackered that it's just a distant memory. They then change at lightning speed–growing rapidly and doing new and different things. They're crawling in the blink of an eye, then walking, talking, going to school, then writing and reading. One minute you're cute first-time parents with an adorable tiny baby, then faster than you can say 'powdered infant formula', you're already a seasoned mum and dad with mini person in tow. The size of your kids really reflect your age. By the time you've got an annoying teenager or two, most probably towering over you, there's no escaping the fact that you've spent a large chunk of your life parenting, stressed out and wondering where your life disappeared.

There were very few clouds in the sky. It looked like it was going to be a nice day. The weather was improving, as predicted.

Suzy and I rushed the rest of the way to school and made it just as the bell rang. I bent down and gave her a kiss. She hugged me tightly, then waved continuously as she disappeared up the steps and into the building. She'd clearly enjoyed me dropping her off at school. So had I. It was heartwarming. I need to do it more often.

I walked to the High Street. The jewellers was open, so I went in. I hoped to God that no one in there recognised me, or knew Fiona. There was only an elderly gentleman, who appeared to be the owner. I asked for a simple gold ring. He pulled out a drawer from under the counter and I tried a few on. It was pretty obvious from the mark on my left hand what I was up to. I found a suitable ring and enquired about the price. It was £175. I asked if he had anything cheaper, as I didn't want to waste that much money if I managed to recover my original ring. He looked at me rather suspiciously and shook his head, so I came clean with him, though I missed out the bit about the prostitute. He smiled and said that he'd keep the ring for me until 6:00pm. I'd have to leave work a little earlier to get back in time.

With a plan in place, I headed to the station. I'd just missed a train up to London and I had to wait another half an hour, so I loitered about outside. There's a barbers next door. I was definitely need of a haircut. If I was going out with trendy Jason then I didn't want too look like a pikey. The place was empty, so I went in.

I'd not been too the hairdressers for ages, having given up on my hair a while ago. I used to take great care of it, having a regular trim and applying all sorts of products. In recent years I've just cut it myself with clippers, then let it slowly grow back into an unruly mop.

The barber asked what I wanted. I had no idea, so I let him get on with it. I ended up with a short, modern-looking cut—neat at the sides and back and ruffled up top. My head felt lighter and I looked younger. It literally took several years off me compared to my usual messy barnet. I was pleasantly surprised.

I caught the next train up to town, feeling refreshed. I enquired about my ring at the main station. It hadn't been handed in. I also asked at the Underground. They gave me a number to call. I dialled it on my way to the sauna, but I ended up in a never-ending queue.

The sauna was closed, as I'd expected. I knocked a few times just in case, but there was no reply. I continued walking along the street towards work, until I heard someone calling after me...I stopped and turned to see a woman leaning out of the sauna door—it was Lucky. She was wearing jeans and a t-shirt. I didn't recognise her at first.

I followed her back into the building and we stood at the foot of the stairs. She had a cloth in her hand, as if she'd been cleaning. I hadn't expected her to answer the door. I felt a bit embarrassed as I asked whether anyone had found a ring. "So yer married then?" she replied, laughing a little. I nodded. "Aye it's here" she said, reaching under the counter and producing my lost ring.

I couldn't believe it! I was overjoyed. I put it back on my finger immediately and thanked her profusely. I wanted to hug her, but I didn't know whether it was appropriate. "Dey don't call me Lucky fer nuthin!" she joked. "How can I repay you?" I asked. "How about yer boi me brekkie?" she suggested, after a pause, "Oive been working since seven." I'd been hoping to head on into work, but I definitely owed Lucky one, so I agreed.

We left the sauna and headed to a shabby looking greasy spoon just down the road. We sat at a table with orange moulded plastic seats that were fixed to the floor. A rather haggard looking waitress took our order. Lucky asked for a full English breakfast and I ordered a coffee. "Me name's actually Lucy" she said voluntarily, while fishing the tea-bag from her cup. I stretched my arm across the table and shook her hand. "Nice to meet you...Lucky Lucy" I replied. She smiled.

The conversation flowed naturally, as the night before. Lucy was very chatty and I felt relaxed in her company. She explained that she also cleans the sauna in the mornings. She needs the extra cash as she's saving up to go travelling.

Despite her many tattoos, Lucy had an otherwise angelic quality, which made for an interesting combination. Her bright red hair was tied up and she was wearing a tight t-shirt and skinny jeans. Looking at her across the table, it occurred to me that I'd seen her butt naked and felt her bare skin against mine. It was a little odd.

I offered another apology for last night. I explained that it wasn't that I didn't find her attractive. I also told her about Fiona. She seemed touched that I'd wanted to stay faithful. Many of her customers were married men, she explained. "I could give ya a blow job if yer like...Dat's not cheatin" she suggested cheekily, laughing aloud. She then grabbed my mobile off the table and punched in her number. A few seconds later her phone rang from inside her jeans pocket and she hung up. "Dere, now yer have moi number. In case yer need me" she said, chuckling again.

The absurdity of the situation struck me— there I was sitting a greasy café in London, with a prostitute, on a Thursday morning, when I should've been at work. She'd finished her breakfast, so I payed, thanked her again for finding my ring and we parted company.

I carried on into work. I stopped just short of the office to gather myself. The plaza was bathed in sunlight. I lifted my head to the sky, closed my eyes and soaked it up for a moment. I was feeling revitalised and ready to crack on where I'd finished when I left work late last night. I needed to act as if I'd just been ill, then I had to catch up with the half day's work that I'd missed. I also needed to submit my proposal for tomorrow. I had a fair bit to do.

I checked in with the secretary and filled out a sickness form, then went upstairs to see the guys. I'd not missed much. Mark and Ryan were on site again, making some minor repairs to a system we'd recently installed at an office in East London. Clare and Darius were busy with paperwork.

Clare had a few queries for me, so she wheeled her chair over to my desk to discuss them. She was finally wearing her skirt-suit, with her legs on show. They're nearly as fine as Scarlet's–long and smooth with slender ankles and thighs. I've really gotten into women's legs of recent. It used to be tits and faces that interested me the most, but now it's legs and bums...and fannies of course. I briefly wondered whether Clare shaves her pussy, like Lucy. Apparently it's quite common these days, not just in pornos. She's very meticulous and well presented, so I'm sure that she keeps it neat down there. But I can't imagine her taking it all off. It seems too hardcore.

I gave Clare the Birmingham proposal to proof-read. She was very complimentary about it and excited by our prospects. I'd re-read it myself on the train and was also pleasantly surprised at how it sounded. We definitely have a good chance of winning the job. There had been no further rumours from Team Twatface, though I'd seen TF himself lurking around. Clare found a few typos, which I corrected before pinging it over to the boss with a quick covering email.

With that out of the way, I ploughed headlong into my inbox and beat seven shades of shit out of the fucker, scything it down to one measly screen of messages. I then sat at my desk all afternoon, making good progress on a range of issues—speaking to an office in Acton about their fire training needs; looking over a layout for a member of another team; researching a new alarm product that's just come on the market.

Jason texted again to ask about beers. I'd forgotten to get back to him. I was suddenly feeling more up for it. Fiona's right, I need to go out more often. Jason and I had lots to catch up on, so I agreed to meet him. We exchanged a few messages over the course of the afternoon, mostly about where to go. He wanted to take me to a trendy bar in the East-End. I fancied a central London pub instead. We agreed to meet in the pub, then perhaps head to the bar later on, depending upon how late I stayed out.

I got an email from the boss' PA around 4:00pm, saying that he'd give the document a look for tomorrow. She confirmed that the presentations would start at 10:00am. All was set. I was suddenly feeling quite confident about my chances.

I changed in the office loos after work. I don't really have many decent going-out clothes these days. My wardrobe consists mainly of a few pairs of scruffy jeans, sweatshirts and t-shirts. At least my new haircut looked good. It really made a difference to my appearance.

The streets of central London were alive with activity. It was rush hour, but there was a positive vibe in the air. The upturn in the weather has put a smile on peoples' faces. Office workers hung outside pubs and bars drinking and smoking. Others rushed off home, perhaps to enjoy the warm evening in the garden or the park. I love London when it's like this. It rubs off on me and I remember the fun times that Fiona and I had in the city after university–running around town, partying and soaking up the excitement of the Capital.

I met up with Jason at one of my favourite haunts from that period–an old pub hidden behind Camden Town Hall. We used to score weed in there, off a guy called Magic Mike. It's changed owners since then, but it still has the same run-down decor and edgy atmosphere. I was sure I recognised one of the locals propping up the bar, from our visits to the place all those years ago. I ordered a pint of ale and sat in the corner waiting for Jason.

He appeared shortly afterwards. He looked no different than the last time I'd seen him. He always dresses as you'd expect a DJ or a perhaps a nightclub promoter to dress–somewhat casual, but not scruffy. He never needs to don a suit, nor smart trousers and a shirt. His clothes are invariably urban designer gear or sportswear. It makes him look somewhat younger than he actually is.

Fiona and I first met Jason at a party in an disused warehouse near Kings Cross Station. We'd just moved up to London and I was still really into clubbing. I dragged her along to hear a disc-jockey that I was into. Jason was also down there with his girlfriend Madeline, and we got talking in the chill-out room. We hung out regularly for several years after that, though he split up with Madeline soon afterwards. He never seems to stay with the same girl for more than a few months.

Jason was also into house music and was already playing records at some small parties. He would entertain us back at his flat after nights out, with his amazing record collection and his silky skills. All number of messed up punters would end up round his place, keeping the party going until the early hours.

Whenever we meet up, however long it has been since I last saw him, it always reminds of that fun period. They were great times—definitely some of the best. I often long for those days, when Fiona and I used to stay out 'till dawn and meet all manner of interesting characters in night-time London. It felt so adventurous after our relatively sheltered university years in Leicester.

While life has now changed considerably for us, Jason has more or less carried on doing the same thing since then. He still has the same flat in North London and he's never with the same woman for very long.

It was great to see him. We sunk a few beers and shared our respective stories. I filled Jason in on life outside London and the stress of commuting. I also mentioned the possible promotion at work and my problems with Twatface. He agreed that TF sounds like a complete tosser.

I enquired about Jason's recent adventures in the dance music scene. Though I lost touch myself many years ago, I always enjoy his stories of the glamorous yet seedy goings-on. He's recently DJ'ed at a few different places in London, but he reckons that that the scene has changed, the music has changed, and the people have also changed. He's still enjoying it and making a living, of a sort, but it's lost its appeal somewhat. It's not the same as the good old days, when we first used to hang out, he says. We reminisced about a few particularly fun nights and the hilarious shenanigans we got up to.

I asked Jason about his love life. He's recently split up with a 26 year old blonde. He showed me pictures of her on his phone. She looked hot. He never has any problems getting hold of chicks–they seem to flock after him. He'd been with the latest one for six months, which was a long time for him. He'd started thinking that she might be 'the one', but as he fell in love and opened up to her, she lost interest and things went downhill. His previous relationships have followed a similar pattern. Young women like him because he's a DJ and he has connections. This makes it easy to bed them, but few are up for a commitment. They're mostly interested in going out and getting wasted instead. Having spent over half his life partying, Jason reckons that he's ready to settle down. He wants to meet a nice girl. One that doesn't drink too much and do too many drugs. I sympathise with him a little...but not the part about screwing 20-somethings.

He enquired about Fiona and I, so I opened up to him, painting an equally honest picture of married life with kids and the stresses it puts on a relationship. I complained about the sex drying up and about the fantasies that often plague me. I also told him about the mess I'd gotten into last night. There are few people that I can share something like that with. He laughed like hell, almost spitting out his beer when I got the part about losing the ring and Fiona waiting up for me. I have to admit that it's pretty hilarious. I really had a close shave there!

Though we're similar-aged, our plights couldn't be more different these days. The grass also appears distinctly greener on the other side. I wouldn't mind swapping positions with Jason for a night or two, just to break the cycle of boredom and familiarity, and live a little. He admitted that he's always been a bit envious that I found the right woman early on, and that I stuck with her. He also wants kids.

Jason spoke highly of Fiona, pointing out that she never stopped me doing what I wanted during those crazy days in London, and that she never acted jealous when Jason and I hung out alone, even though there were often women involved.

He brought up the subject of our holiday in Ibiza...It was meant to be a couples' thing. Fiona and I were heading out with Jason and one of his girlfriends for a beach holiday, and to check out the famous nightlife. But they split up just weeks before—his decision this time—and mate of his called Alex came instead. It therefore ended up less of a couples' holiday and more of a lad's trip, with Fiona tagging along as the lone female. She took it very well, despite having to sit out a few of the crazier club nights and stay at the apartment on her own.

One day, the four of us visited a cove where an after-party was taking place. Us lads had been up all night, so Fiona drove us there in our shitty rental car. We lay on the sand, drinking, sunbathing and recovering from the night before.

Several women on the beach had their tits out, which added to the appeal of the place. I enquired, jokingly, whether Fiona was going to follow suit. Sensing that I was showing off in front of Jason and Alex, she called my bluff by asking them whether they would mind. They didn't of course, so a little while later, when no one was looking, she unclipped her bikini top and took it off...It was very sexy, particularly in our wasted state. I was very proud, as she had great breasts. I remember taking a topless photo of her.

Jason cheekily admitted that that day remains his abiding memory of the Ibiza holiday. I remarked that Fiona still has good tits, particularly given that she's had two kids. He asked me whether she still gets them out at the beach. Unfortunately that was one of the only times. He reckons that I should encourage her more, like in Ibiza. It's true, I've not asked her again. Maybe she wants me too? I wondered whether she'd still do things like that, if I suggested it. I'd like her to shave her muff off, like Lucy. That would be very hot.

I texted Fiona while I was having a piss, telling her that I'd really enjoyed last night.

Jason and I chatted about various friends that we used to know and what they're up to now. He's kept in touch with more people than I have. I occasionally look at what my old mates and acquaintances are up to, on the Web. But I suspect that they only share the good bits. It's not the same as meeting up with them in person, and having a proper conversation.

Fiona and I have consolidated our circle of friends somewhat since having Michael and moving out of London. It's not been intentional. It's just that it's been harder to stay in proper contact with as many people as before. We've lost touch with a quite a few folk, but also gained some new friends, out in Essex. The move actually brought us closer to one couple that we knew from university, who settled down early on and have lived in the area for years.

The small core group of old friends, with which we were very much entwined during in our London years, have mostly remained in the city, but have spread out to different parts of the Capital, in their search for affordable accommodation. They almost never get together as a group anymore, though Jason makes the effort to see most of them from time to time. Most have got kids, houses, mortgages, and like us, are 40 or thereabouts.

Jason filled me in on some of the gossip that hadn't been posted on the Internet. Pete and Mary, a couple that we once saw a lot of, have recently parted company. Pete was always a bit of a bright spark and ended up lecturing at university. Mary was also very driven and held down a good job in HR, while having kids. This much I already knew from the pictures and information they post from time to time. However, Jason explained that Pete had had an affair with one of his students, about a year ago. He and Mary recently split up over it and have now been living apart for several months. It was sad to hear. Jason reckons that the student isn't all that hot–just younger and different to Mary, I guess.

The most shocking news, however, was that Luther, a great friend of ours, and a massive character from the old days, had suffered some sort of breakdown. It happened a couple of years ago, which shows how long I'd not seen Jason. No one knows the cause exactly; it seems that he simply couldn't cope with life, though he'd always taken a lot of drugs. He disappeared suddenly. He just gave up his job and his flat without telling anybody, not even his girlfriend, and left the country. He went east to India and Vietnam, to find himself. It was a big worry for his family and close friends. He simply took off one day, leaving a letter for his girlfriend, explaining that he needed some space. No one heard from him for a year and a half. He's now back in the country, at least temporarily, but he's a changed person, apparently. Jason's seen him.

It was strangely comforting to hear about Luther's situation. I definitely find it hard to cope myself at times. Monday was a good example. The stress of everyday life just gets to me. Sometimes I wish that there was a pause button that I could press. That way I could relax and sort my head out, without things continually piling up, and time whizzing by. I'm always far too busy dealing with the day-to-day stuff to get a chance to straighten myself out. Perhaps that's how Luther felt? I've never contemplated disappearing though. It'd cause too much pain and too much mess.

Our conversation about Luther, Pete and Mary was a brief and somewhat solemn interlude in what was a very enjoyable catch-up with Jason. We sunk quite a few beers and laughed a lot. He then suggested that we check out the bar that he had in mind. Some friends of his were also going—three ladies. I didn't want to stay too late on account of my presentation tomorrow, but I was feeling rather upbeat, and also a little drunk. I figured that I could get the 11:18 or 11:48pm train home, so I'd be back for a quarter past midnight at the latest.

We headed to East London. It's a part of the city that I thought I knew well, but it's now changed beyond recognition. We used to frequent a few dingy establishments there in the past, amidst shoe factories and various run down municipal buildings. The place used to be a wasteland after dark, save for the constant rush of traffic passing directly through it and the occasional dodgy character, also on their way to somewhere else. These days it's a pulsating, albeit still very industrial-looking region, crammed with bars and clubs, where London's in-crowd party all nights of the week. I was shocked. It *really* had been a long time since I'd been out!

Jason led me to the bar. It was decidedly plush and glamorous compared to the pub. I felt very under-dressed. There were no hand-pulled ales in sight, so I settled for a gin-and-tonic. We then found Jason's friends, who were sitting on some sofas by a low table. They had to be in their mid to late 20's. All were dressed up nicely and two of them were pretty hot. Jason introduced me and I tried to strike up conversation with the one nearest to me—an Asian girl—but she was rather offish.

The bar felt quite sterile after the cozy pub. It was also pretty empty at that point. There was a DJ in the corner, who appeared to be playing off a laptop. I've just about gotten used to people using CDs instead of records, but a computer? Surely there's no skill involved in that? I wasn't particularly impressed with the music he was playing. All his tunes sounded the same—just a kick drum and a bland bass line, with some American diva warbling over the top. It was like stuff that I'd heard at least 15 years earlier, and I didn't like then.

I began to feel a little uncomfortable and out of place. Jason was busy talking to his mates. They all seemed to be enjoying themselves—nodding their heads and looking at the DJ.

The girls went off to the toilets and Jason shuffled over to speak to me. I gave him my honest assessment of the bar and the music. He called me a miserable bastard, then slipped something into my hand and added "This'll cheer you up." It was a small bag of white powder, which appeared to be cocaine. I might have guessed it. I thought he'd seemed a little too wide-eyed and sprightly for a Thursday night. He explained that the girls were on it as well. They must've been in the bogs at that moment, taking some.

I gave the bag straight back to him. I'd stopped taking drugs a long time ago and I didn't exactly feel like starting again. I did a fair amount of coke, E's and a range of other stuff in my 20's and early 30's. It never really developed into a problem, but after years of casual recreational use, I just drifted out of that scene. Fiona has never been that much into drugs, so it was easy enough to give up once we settled down and had kids. As I stopped going out, I found that I didn't need them any more.

The girls returned from the loos. They looked as if they'd taken something. They sat down again and I ended up next to a different one—a brunette with big tits. She seemed a little friendlier than her mate. I smiled and we got chatting.

Her name was Annette. She knew Jason through the music scene, as I'd expected. She and her mates were there to check the DJ. Apparently he's particularly hot at the moment. She was bopping her head and tapping her foot, while talking constantly about various clubs and genres, none of which meant anything to me. It was clear that she was off her face; she had an extreme case of 'motor-mouth'.

Though Annette was rather tasty, I found her a little boring after a while. She didn't have much to say for herself. I tried a few times to divert the conversation onto a topic other than dance music, but failed. It might have been her age, or because she was on coke, or perhaps both. Either way, we were on a different level

I slowly warmed to the prospect of trying some of Jason's stuff. It was a ludicrous idea, to be taking class-A drugs at age 39.99, and after such a long break. But like Wednesday night, I felt a rush of excitement and naughtiness at the thought of letting go and doing something a little out of the ordinary.

There's no way I want to be taking drugs in my 40's, so it was perhaps my last chance to have a final dabble. I didn't want to get wrecked the night before my presentation, but I reckoned that I could just do one small line, to put me on the same page as the other four. I could then have a couple more drinks and head home.

I asked Jason for the bag and popped to the gents. I locked myself in one of the cubicles. The whole cocaine ritual suddenly came flooding back to me, as if I'd done it just yesterday—finding a flat, dry surface; shaking out some powder; crushing and chopping it up with a credit card; quietly rolling up banknote and snorting it in one go, while flushing the loo to hide the sound. I'd deftly performed the same sequence of actions many times in the distant past, in all number of grimy conveniences, across the city.

I paused briefly with a rather modest line of coke laid out on the toilet cistern, wondering whether it was the right thing to be doing on a Thursday night, what with the Birmingham thing tomorrow. But there were other people outside, waiting to use the toilet, so I bent down and did it...

The bar had changed when I exited the gents. It seemed smaller and more crowded. I was feeling the drugs already—my senses had sharpened and there was a steely, numb feeling at the back of my throat. I sat down on the sofa and handed the bag back to Jason. He winked at me.

I'd forgotten how much I love cocaine. An amazing clarity came over me. The music even sounded better. It was strong stuff; not like the rubbish we used to take. Either that or I was just not used to it.

As the coke did its magic and I felt more relaxed and confident, I struck up conversation again with Annette. I grabbed hold of the pulpit myself this time and waxed lyrical about the 'good old days' when Jason and I used to go clubbing. I recalled a few particularly great parties that I'd been to and the now-famous DJs that I'd seen, when they were in there prime. I was showing off, but it felt good for a moment.

Annette seemed rather impressed. She sat forward and listened to me across the table, while chewing a lot and nodding to the music. I felt almost cool all of a sudden. I certainly *used* to be trendy and in-the-know. These days I wouldn't know one record or DJ from another. The last CD I bought, perhaps a year ago, was some cheesy pop rubbish that I grabbed at a supermarket counter. Annette wouldn't have been impressed. Luckily she didn't ask what I do for a living. It would've surely killed the conversation.

I checked my phone. It was 10:00pm. Fiona had replied to my text. She said that last night had been great for her too. It was good to hear. I feel like our sex life might be on the mend. I just have to keep her interested and excite her a little more. In a rush of confidence, I texted that I wanted to 'fuck' her when I got back. It felt very raunchy to put it so bluntly. I got a text straight back from her with a smiley face. It was a good response.

I felt like I might be rediscovering my mojo. I'm definitely feeling more confident around women all of a sudden and less of a nervous wreck. I sensed it this morning with Lucky. I was relaxed in her company and I was able to make her laugh. I also had no problem holding Annette's attention. I'd not felt like this in a while. It was quite intoxicating. The coke definitely helped. If Scarlet had strolled into the bar at that moment, I might have tried to chat her up, just for the hell of it.

A while later the three girls took to the small dance-floor and beckoned Jason and I along. I'd not danced in the longest time. It felt good. The coke seemed to be urging my limbs to move. We boogied in front of the DJ booth. It was just like old times. Jason was right about the bar, it really was kicking! I gave him the thumbs up and he grinned back.

I found myself dancing near Annette. She smiled, while shimmying in my direction. I smiled back and we had a little dance together. Our bodies didn't touch, but she was definitely mine for a few minutes. It sent my pulse racing. Her huge tits bobbed up and down and I could see straight into her cleavage as she gyrated in front of me. She didn't seem to be wearing a bra.

Out of the corner of my eye I spotted someone at the edge of the dance-floor, staring straight at me. Someone I recognised. I did a massive double-take as I realised who it was...Terry Fucking Francis! I could *not* fucking believe it!..Twatface was definitely the last person in the world I'd expected to see at that moment. He was also the last person I wanted to bump into, except perhaps Fiona. What were the chances?

He was standing alongside another guy, with a drink in his hand, giving me one of his evil smirky looks that I despise. I leant over and pointed him out to Jason. "Looks like a cunt" Jason commented.

TF then strolled over and approached me. "Aren't you a bit old for this place?" he shouted over the music, standing a metre or so away. I was still feeling a foot taller due to the coke, so I squared up to him and replied "Shouldn't you be at home with your new-born baby?" He scoffed, then turned and wandered back to his mate—a podgy looking prat with trendy floppy hair—and they disappeared.

Twatface has just had a kid with a lass from work called Sandrine. She was the best-looking chick in the office by a fair distance. He moved in on her shortly after he joined the firm, which of course made her off limits. He used to go on about how much he hated kids, calling them 'friend thieves'—because they steal your mates—but now he acts like he's the first man to ever father a child. I reckon that he's happy that Sandrine is stuck at home. The new baby doesn't appear to stop him going out after work in the middle of the week.

A little while longer, I noticed that the smarmy fucker had reappeared. I'd hoped that he'd left. He and his mate were now dancing too. The dance-floor was pretty small, so he inevitably ended up near us. He smirked at me again and moved towards Annette. He must have seen me dancing with her earlier. He was trying to piss me off.

He started dancing directly behind her. She noticed him, then moved away disgust. His gormless pal was grinning, which egged him on further. He then approached her again and rubbed against her ass in a lurid manner. He seemed determined to wind me up. I've seen TF say and do all number of cringeworthy things over the years, but this was a step too far. I'd been having a good time with Jason and his friends and he was really getting on my nerves.

As he continued to hit on Annette, I felt the full force of my almighty hatred for him well up inside me...It eventually peaked and I snapped. I went at him like a wild animal, unable to control myself.

My first punch caught him on the side of his head. It felt really hard, like a rock. It took him by surprise. As he turned to face me, I landed about three more punches on him in quick succession. It all happened very suddenly. My arms felt detached from my body, thrashing about doing their own thing. TF just stood there absorbing the impact with his mellon, which flopped back and forth as they hit.

The crowd parted seconds later and a gargantuan black bouncer grabbed the two of us and dragged us out of the bar, one in each hand. He ejected us through the emergency exit and into a dark back-alley.

We looked at each other for a moment, then TF suddenly lunged at me, cursing. He punched me in the mouth, then on the ear. I tried to fight back, but I didn't have a chance to readjust myself.

Luckily the doors flew open again and Jason rushed out. Seeing TF was upon me, he spun him around with one hand and landed the most almighty right-hook straight on his nose with the other. There was a distinct crunching sound as TF's septum shattered and his nose splatted across his face. The force sent him flying onto the ground.

A moment of silence followed, before TF got up, groaning and holding his face, with blood pouring out between his fingers. Noticing Jason coming in for more, he ran off down the alley and disappeared into the night.

His floppy-haired friend then emerged from the bar. He saw the two of us and fled immediately. I instinctively stuck out a leg and tripped him as he passed. He slapped helplessly against the cobbled street, letting out a comedy "Ooof!", before also desperately scrambling away.

I dusted myself down. I was shaking from the rush of adrenaline and, of course, the coke. There was no chance of me getting back into the bar, so we went to a nearby pub.

Though I'd taken a few punches, we'd definitely come out on top, mostly thanks to Jason. We sat at the bar and toasted our victory with a pint. We recalled the details of the fight, laughing about Twatface's nose splitting and his mate hitting the deck. I'd not punched anyone since I was at school. I was surprised with myself. It was strangely satisfying to inflict pain on another human being, especially TF. I'd secretly wanted to hit him for years. It'd been a natural reaction to protect Annette. He'd definitely deserved it.

Jason offered me some more coke. I was still feeling the effects of the first line, but in my victorious mood, I accepted. The stuff is just so damn moreish. He had a hit too and we sat in the pub a little longer, feeling the buzz.

We agreed that it had been great to see each other and that we need to do it more often. Jason asked again about my plans for Sunday. "You've got to celebrate your fortieth" he insisted. I agreed that it would be a pity to let it pass without ceremony. "Great, so you're having a party!" he suggested, "I'll bring some music." It seemed like a great idea all of a sudden, in my uplifted state of mind, so I agreed.

Jason headed back to the bar to the girls, who'd been texting him since the fight. I bid him good night and made my way to the nearest Tube station. I floated my way across London, off my head. The train journey back was also a bit if a blur. There were very few people in the carriage, so I slumped in seat of four, hogging them all, as the train trundled along the route I take every day to and from work. It seemed very different.

It'd been another eventful day. The last week of my 40's was now shaping up nicely. I could finally feel the blood pumping in my veins again. It was as if I was coming back to life, after a laying in a half-coma for an indeterminable length of time. I caught a glimpse of myself in the train window. I was a bit bloodied, but I looked good. The haircut had been a good idea. I smiled at my reflection, happy to see myself for once.

Fiona was shocked when I got in. I told her about the fight with TF. I reckoned that I'd probably screwed my chances of getting promoted. Twatface might even press charges. But I didn't care at that moment. I felt like a hero returning from battle.

She loved my new haircut. She cleaned me up in the bathroom. I had a split lip and I'd smeared the blood across my cheek with my hand. It looked worse than it actually was. I filled her in on Jason's news and the gossip he'd shared with me. I also mentioned the party. She liked the idea.

Fiona said that she'd loved my text. Remembering what I had written, I leant forward and kissed her. We started snogging, there in the bathroom. I slid my hand down her pyjamas and felt her pussy. It was quite hairy. I asked her whether she'd shave it off for me some day. She looked a little put out at first, but then replied "D'you like that?" I nodded.

We moved to the bedroom. Fiona undid my jeans and got my cock out. It was shrivelled from the coke, but it grew immediately as she touched it. She then sucked me. She'd not given me a blow-job for years. The sensation of her warm, moist mouth on my helmet was out of this world! It felt like losing my virginity all over again. It was almost *too* good. I felt myself coming, so I pulled Fiona's head away from my crotch, tore of her pyjamas and fucked her, as I'd promised.

I was so turned on that I had to think of something else to stop myself ejaculating. I thought about fire alarms, but it didn't work. I then imagined myself punching TF at the bar. This did the trick. I humped Fiona rhythmically, as my fists hit his skull—harder and harder, faster and faster. It was a very violent shag. She seemed to love it.

I can't remember the last time we'd had sex two nights in row. Perhaps before we were married? It was the perfect ending to an extremely enjoyable and very crazy night.

I slept immediately.

Friday
39 years, 363 days

I was woken by the sun streaming into the bedroom. We'd forgotten to close the curtains last night. I was naked and there were clothes strewn across the floor. Fiona was still fast asleep.

I'd woken before my alarm for once. I didn't feel too sleepy, so I leaned over and cancelled it. I'd drunk a fair bit of alcohol last night, but I didn't feel groggy. I appeared to be experiencing the after effects of the drugs. I lay there for a bit, staring at the ceiling and listening to the birds singing outside.

I wasn't sure what awaited me at work. Were the presentations still going to be on? If so, then I needed to nail my talk in order to stand a chance of getting the job. If Twatface had reported my violent behaviour, then the promotion might be the least of my worries. I might be facing some sort of disciplinary process. Either way, today was going to be a day of reckoning for me. I might be promoted, sacked, or perhaps neither.

It'd definitely been a mistake to get so fucked last night. But I'd had a lot of fun and I still felt perked up, despite getting to bed late. I smiled as I recalled punching TF. If I didn't get the promotion, or if I ended up losing my job, then at least Jason and I had given him his comeuppance.

I heard Suzy and Michael playing, so I got up too. My body was aching, particularly my jaw and my right fist, which was swollen. The kids were in their pyjamas playing Lego. The cat lay beside the pile of plastic bricks, hoping for a stroke.

I showered, washing last night's semen from my body. I noticed that my knob had returned to its normal size, after the coke shrinkage. In fact it looked quite big.

The recent upturn in my sex life is making me appreciate myself a little more. I really gave it to Fiona last night in bed, and she loved it. I started touching my cock with my numb, swollen hand. It felt like someone else was doing it. I fantasised about being pulled off by Annette. Then I imagined her in the shower with me, bending over and facing the wall, with me entering her from behind and her massive jugs hanging down.

I then pictured Fiona on a beach, going topless again. I imagined that Jason and Alex were there too, as in Ibiza, but 18 years later. Fiona asked if it was OK if she took her bikini *bottoms* off this time. The guys didn't mind, so she stood up, pulled them straight down and let them drop onto the sand. To our surprise, she had no pussy hair...The fantasy turned me on so much that I ejaculated onto the shower screen, before I had a chance to grab something to catch the cum.

The kids and I performed our morning drill with aplomb. I couldn't be late today of all days. The weather forecast on the radio predicted a scorcher for the weekend. It still looked good outside, so maybe they'll get it right this time.

Fiona was just up when I went to clean my teeth. We laughed at our clothes littered around the room. It was encouraging evidence that we *can* make it work between us sexually after all these years. I still can't believe that she gave me a blow job last night. I hope it happens again. She wished me luck and I left the house in a decidedly upbeat mood.

I should've brought a copy of my document with me to read on the train, or at least tried to recall what was in it. But I was feeling rather blissed-out and unfocussed. I also wasn't sure whether it would be necessary. Instead, I imagined what I might say if the boss hauled me over the coals for fighting with Twatface. I pictured the two of us in his office, like two schoolboys who'd just had a scrap in the playground. TF would surely point at me and claim "He started it." I'd have no response other than to state that he was being a sleazy piece of shit and he therefore deserved it.

I texted Jason, who I gathered would still be in bed, to say thanks for an excellent night. I confirmed that I'm up for having a party on Sunday and that I wanted him to bring some music along. I also asked whether he could invite Luther, Alex, Pete or any of our old London friends that he still knew. He replied shortly afterwards, saying "Will do. Hilarious evening!"

I finally snapped out of my trance as I approached the office. I began to get a little nervous, but decided to just head straight in and face the music. The receptionist greeted me with a smile. I couldn't sense whether anything was up. I headed upstairs and met Clare, who was in early, as always. She looked concerned when she saw my bruised face and the way that I was holding my injured hand. I told her that I'd fallen down some stairs. She didn't seem to know any different.

Clare had re-read my document and suggested that we go over it straight away. She fixed me a coffee and we headed into one of the meeting rooms. She already knew the proposal inside-out. She walked me through it, with the slides projected on the wall. It was exactly what I needed to get me focussed for the morning's meeting. What a star!

There was no sign of Twatface. His team was gathered on the other side of the office, looking a little worried. It appeared as if he wasn't going to show up. Either that or he was planning some sort of stunt. I didn't say anything.

The two teams headed into the conference room just before 10:00pm. Ryan and Mark had stayed at the office, so they could attend the meeting. Team TF sat on the other side of the long table from us. The boss and two members of senior management were at the far end. They suggested that we should present first, as TF had still not yet arrived.

I felt a sudden rush of nerves and adrenaline as I realised that this was it...I now needed to deliver our pitch for the project.

Clare had already loaded my presentation onto the computer for me. She had also printed out copies of the document. It was a nice touch. She distributed them as I stood in front of the projector screen and gathered myself.

I can't remember much of the 15 minutes that followed. The light from the projector was blinding me, so I could only really see the people sitting nearest to me. Clare's expression told me that it was going well. She was nodding her head and smiling occasionally.

As the slides flashed up on the screen, I managed to recite verbatim the text that I'd planned to go with them. The last minute revision session had worked. By the time I got to the last slide, I actually felt rather confident up there. I wanted to carry on. But Clare started clapping and the rest of the room joined in, so I stopped.

The boss asked me if we'd incorporated any measures for mobility-impaired people. I'd thought that the question might come up. I cited the 'ski-pads' and other evacuation aids that we intended to supply and to provide training on. I'd also earmarked a couple of places in the hospital that could be adapted for use as a fire refuge. He nodded in approval. One of the directors enquired about the portable extinguishers, which was pretty easy to answer. The other team was then given a chance to quiz me on our proposal. No one said a word. They must have been too preoccupied worrying where TF was.

When I returned to my seat and my eyes had adjusted to the darkened room, I noticed that he was still not present. I'd been expecting him to appear at any moment, as if he'd been luring us into a false sense of security. But he clearly wasn't turning up. The boss asked whether one of his team was going to deputise for their missing leader. They looked terrified, as if they too had expected him to walk in at the last minute and save the day.

Mandy, the next most senior member of Team TF, reluctantly got up and headed to the front. She fiddled with the computer for a few minutes, then nervously began.

Mandy is a self-confessed post-feminist bitch. Darius calls her 'Man-dy' because she looks and acts like a man. She and TF make a rather odd couple, what with him being a sexist pig. They seem to feed off each other's nastiness. He treats her like a bloke, which she probably enjoys.

Without Twatface for support, Mandy was completely adrift. Her imaginary cock had shrunk to the size of a pea and retracted back inside her.

While it wasn't her fault that her team leader hadn't turned up, I don't think that anyone felt much sympathy for her. Her presentation was well and truly gash.

If it was the latest version of TF's proposal that she was fumbling her way through, then he must've still been a way off finishing it. He was probably expecting to wing his way through the pitch, then charm the bosses at the interview with his smarmy corporate drivel. Mandy's not in the same league as TF when it comes to bullshitting. She was like a rabbit in the headlights. The whole room breathed a sigh of relief when she finally stopped gibbering.

The panel went pretty easy on her during questions. I also resisted the temptation to embarrass her further. Not Clare however, who tore her to shreds over the Regs. She citied the obvious bits of legislation that hadn't been considered in their flimsy plan. Mandy had no leg to stand on. I was gobsmacked!

The two teams were allowed to disperse, so that the interviews could begin. I left the room while Mandy went first. I was feeling a little drained, after the adrenaline rush of presenting. Clare fixed me a strong coffee. I wondered briefly about TF. Where the hell was he? Jason hadn't hit him that hard. Maybe something else had happened to him after he fled? He could also have been down the police station or on the phone to a solicitor.

Mandy appeared shortly afterwards, looking rather sullen. She told me to go in. I knew at that point that we'd won.

I was right. The boss congratulated me. He was unusually complimentary. It felt like he was finally treating me seriously. One of the directors, Bastard Barry, asked whether I was ready for the promotion and the extra responsibilities that it entailed, such as joining the Fire Emergency Response Team or 'FERT'. I confirmed that I was indeed very much up for it, and in fact relishing the opportunity.

Buoyed by the news that we'd won the project, I then delivered a monologue about how passionate I feel about fire safety and protecting lives and property. It was the kind of spiel that they like to hear. The type that TF probably reels off at meetings when he is trying to act like he cares. Some of it was straight out of magazines that I've read in the coffee room. I think I might have even paraphrased the gumpf on our own website. I referred to my many years of experience with the company, working on site, in the office and managing my own team. I pointed out that I'm familiar with a broad spectrum of the firm's activities.

I was blowing my own trumpet for once. It felt good. I needed to show the boss and his cronies that I *could* be confident in my own abilities.

I wrapped up my lengthy reply by stating that I'm ready to serve the company for many years to come and that I look forward to "Playing an active role in keeping us at the forefront of the Capital's fire and safety management sector." The last bit was 24-carat bullshit of the purest variety known to man. I almost couldn't believe I'd said it.

The boss congratulated me and said that he'll set up a meeting for next Tuesday, to discuss the finer points of my new role. He then leant over and shook my hand. I instinctively held out my right hand to meet his. It was still rather fat and immobile. He clocked it, then winked at me. It was as if he knew what I had been up to last night. I thanked him and the rest of the panel, then left the room.

The guys were pretty jubilant when I told them that we'd been assigned to the project. Clare whooped and gave me a hug. Our success had also been down to her, as well as perhaps Jason's right-hook.

It was lunchtime, so I invited them to the pub. I called Fiona on our way across the plaza, which was bathed in warm midday sun. She was in the middle of a lesson. She sounded very pleased for me. "Well done darling!" she said, as she hung up. She hadn't called me 'darling' in a while. It was lovely.

We grabbed a booth in a large pub, not far from the office, and toasted our success with drinks and grub. Mark and Darius put away several pints between them. I announced that I am going to be 40 on Sunday and invited everyone to the party. The lads ribbed me about my age.

Clare sat next to me on the bench. She was still very excited. She'd really surprised me at the presentations. I'd never seen that aggressive, competitive side of her before. Perhaps she's not the shy girl that she appears to be? She had her skirt-suit on again, with her legs on show. It has a split up the side. It was hard not to look.

I popped into a shop on the plaza on my way back to the office. As I passed one of the cafés, I heard someone call out my name. The voice didn't sound familiar. I turned to see a largish woman at one of the outside tables, standing up and waving at me. I didn't recognise her. She repeated my name again, so I smiled, to confirm that it was indeed me. *"Sue Armitage"* she said. It didn't mean anything to me. *"Sue?..Sue Francis?"*, she corrected herself, seeing the confused look on my face..."Fuck!" I replied in shock, "I mean, fuck me! How are you?". It was Sue, my first love; the girl who dumped me when I started uni. I couldn't believe it! She looked fucking awful.

It took me completely by surprise. One minute I was heading back to the office, thinking about my promotion and the weekend ahead, then the next I was confronted with my ex-girlfriend, who I'd not seen since I was 18.

I went over to greet her, still unable to believe my eyes. She leant forward and offered me a kiss on the cheek. I obliged, then sat down with her at the table.

I'd always hoped that I'd bump into her some day. I'd imagined what I'd say and how I'd feel. I'd gone over it in my mind, literally hundreds of times, especially in the first few years. But I never saw her again after that first fateful summer break, when she delivered the unfortunate news that we were to part. Sue's parents moved to another town, so I never got the opportunity to see her in those following months. I didn't get the chance to understand why she'd kicked me into touch. It made it all the more painful.

That moment had now come; there she was in front of me, though looking very different. She's now a woman, in her late 30's, not the schoolgirl I once loved. She was decidedly rotund and haggard. It was hard to imagine that I was looking at the same woman.

I was a little nervous. It took me a moment to regain my senses. I tried to think what I'd planned to say to her and how I'd intended to act. I couldn't remember. I tried to let her do the talking, as I pulled myself together.

"How *are* you" she said. "I'm very good" I replied, smiling. "You look well", she continued. I resisted the temptation to return her the compliment. She didn't look great. This wasn't how it was meant to be. I'd always imagined meeting Sue the sexy 16 year-old, not the Sue of 22 years later. It was a big let down.

She filled me in on the rest of her story, while lighting up a cigarette and pulling hard on it. She's had a rough time by the sound of it. She went to uni too, in Cardiff. She met a guy there and had a kid by the time she was 20. They got married, but then split up. She brought up her son on her own and spent many years alone. She then met someone else in her early 30's, but this too ended badly. She's been living back with her parents for the last five years and is currently looking for work.

Sue asked me what I'd been up to. I didn't know where to start, given that I'd last seen her over half my life ago. I gave her a quick synopsis– meeting Fiona a year after she finished with me; graduating from Leicester; moving to London; getting married; getting a proper job; having Suzy; having Michael; moving to Essex; commuting back and forth to the city; getting promoted. I guess it sounded decidedly rosier than Sue's adult years. She seemed happy for me.

I should have felt vindicated. I'd always hoped that I'd gain the upper hand after she broke my heart. Instead, I just felt sorry for her.

Sue then mentioned 'Us', all those moons ago. She recalled a few adventures that we got up to back then–like the day her Dad caught us getting it on for the first time. It was certainly an important event in my life and hers–the moment we both lost our virginity. But it didn't feel right to be discussing it with Sue, outside a café, after not seeing her for so long.

It was as if she was flirting with me, or at least seeking some confirmation that she was once desirable. She used to be very pretty and full of energy, but it was hard to believe that I was looking at the same person. She's now grey-haired and overweight, with smoker's skin. I sensed a little desperation in her over-friendly approach. I eventually started to feel uncomfortable.

I needed to get back to work, so as the conversation tailed off, I bid Sue farewell. I told her that I'll look her up on the Web, though I doubt I will. "It's Sue *Armitage* now" she informed me again, "I didn't get round to changing it back." She then jumped up to give me goodbye kiss, holding another fag in one hand and her cold coffee in the other. As I leant in across the table to kiss her cheek, I accidentally knocked her arm, spilling coffee down her white blouse.

She cleaned herself off with a paper towel, while I went into the café to get some more. I then left, apologising profusely, while she dabbed at the stain on her large bosom and waved at me with her other hand.

Back at the office I went into the toilets and broke down. It had been emotional to see Sue. A little *too* emotional, on top of last night and the adrenaline rush of the morning's interview

I've lived with a hole in my heart since the day Sue finished with me. I can still remember it clearly–looking out of the window of her house, as she let me have it; feeling more helpless and lost than I'd ever been; knowing that there was nothing that I could do about it. The hole has slowly mended over the years, but a scar has always remained.

I took a while to gather myself. I dried my eyes and splashed my face with water, before going back to my desk.

Clare was still jubilant about the hospital job. Someone had heard that TF had been in an accident of some sort, but he was OK. "Poor little Twatface" said Darius, laughing. I pretended to be concerned, but I was secretly pissing myself. I guess he knew that I'm not stupid enough to tell anyone what really happened. I can't wait to see the state of him. Luckily nobody seemed to make the connection between my injured hand and his unplanned absence.

I took it easy at work in the afternoon. I had a quick meeting with Geoff, the guy in charge of the FERT. He took my mobile number. I'll eventually need to be on call to assist in fire related incidents and work together with the emergency services. It's a role I'll need to learn, which will be interesting.

Aside from that, I emailed a few folk about Sunday. It's quite short notice. If the weather is going to be as good as they're predicting, then people might already have plans for the bank holiday. I invited all the friends that we've been in touch with recently, as well as few with which we haven't. There needs to be a decent crowd, or it'll not be worth having a do.

As I wrapped up for the day, Clare confirmed that she can make it. Mark also said that he'd try and come. I've not invited any work colleagues to our new place. It'll be a first. Let's hope they get on with my mates.

The journey home on a Friday evening is always the most bearable of the week. I usually get a beer for the train back. This evening I felt particularly jubilant because of my promotion. The sun was shining and I was really looking forward to the weekend. I had a spring in my step and a smile on my face.

I noticed a couple of women looking at me as I navigated my way through the busy streets and along the Underground. I guess a smiling person is a rare sight in rush hour London. Still, I felt like a fanny-magnet all of a sudden. I winked at one lass, who seemed to be checking me out. She looked surprised and immediately turned her head.

I stood up on the train with my beer. A guy accidentally stood on my foot as the carriage rocked its way out of London. I might have growled at him any other day, but I was in such a chirpy mood that I didn't react. He apologised and we had a little chat. It was the first time that I'd had a conversation with a stranger on the train in ages. He was a northerner, which probably explains it as they're usually friendlier than folk down south. He was off to see his brother, who'd just moved out to Essex.

A seat eventually became available, so I sat down and relaxed as the train travelled through the Essex countryside. It suddenly ground to a halt a few miles short of my stop, next to a railway siding that we usually fly past on a daily basis. The driver announced that there was a signal problem ahead and we'd therefore remain stationary for a few minutes, until they sorted it. People around me tutted, sighed and complained. Normally I'd have joined in, but for once I didn't particularly care. Instead, I just gazed out of the window at the rows of engines and carriages in the overgrown yard.

There was a mean looking freight train and some old style passenger carriages, from years back, with the clunky type doors. It was pretty interesting.

It got me thinking—now that I'm approaching my 40's, perhaps I ought to find myself a hobby? Maybe not train-spotting, but something else that captures my imagination.

Our neighbour Anthony has recently taken possession of an impressive-looking American chopper. It's quite a beast—all dazzling chrome and chunky machined aluminium parts. He let me sit on it the other day. Motorbikes aren't really my thing, but his enthusiasm was endearing. He's joined a local club already and they're off for the weekend soon. His wife Barbara reckons he's having a mid-life crisis; apparently she hates the thing. I suggested to him that he should get a sidecar and take her with him. "No chance!" he replied, "Then, I'd never get away from her."

I guess that's part of the reason that men of a certain age take up pursuits like motorbiking, golf or fishing—to get them out of the house and away from the missus. I'm not sure I'm ready for that, but maybe in another 10 or 15 years, when the kids are grown up? Then I'll perhaps find myself an obsession that Fiona hates, so we don't get on each other's nerves too much. Anthony's got to be at least 55.

I always used to have a pastime, or at least a keen interest, such as my obsession with dance music. I was really into football when I was a kid. I went to quite a few games with my dad. Perhaps I should get back into it? Maybe I could check out the local team and take Michael along? I've driven past their tiny stadium many times. It looks like they could do with some support. Michael might like it.

I could even do some sport myself? Walking to the train station and back is about the only exercise I do these days. I've put on a few pounds in recent years and I'm not likely to get any thinner as I head towards middle age. Fiona's recently taken up jogging. She reckons that she's lost a stone.

I bought Fiona some flowers from the shop next to the station. She loved them. I hugged the kids, then headed upstairs for a much needed shower. I felt decidedly rank. The after-buzz of last night's coke had worn off and I could feel the alcohol coming out of my pores.

Fiona cooked Mexican, which is one of my favourite meals. The kids love making their own fajitas, though they get in a real mess. We toasted my promotion and looked forward to the weekend ahead. The kids are excited about the party.

Once Suzy and Michael were settled, Fiona and I retired to the lounge. I called my parents in France. I'd not spoken to them for a couple of weeks. They sounded pleased about my promotion. They had Margaret and her family round for dinner, who also live out there. Mum and Dad moved to be nearer to her when they retired. She's married to a Frenchman and they've got three teenage kids, all bilingual.

Mum asked if I had plans for Sunday, so I told her about the party. She said that they were sorry that they wouldn't be with me on my birthday. It's a pity. I don't remember them missing Margaret's 40th. Oh well. As my dad once put it, they're "Living their own lives again", now that they've retired.

Fiona and I opened a bottle of wine. We made a list of the guests that are hopefully coming on Sunday. It looks like there might be a decent enough crowd. I've already received a confirmation text from Nick and Vanessa, the Leicester Uni couple who live in the next town. They've become good friends again, after not seeing them for many years.

As we got talking about various people we used to hang out with, I went into the loft and brought down a box of old photos that have been up there since we moved. I sat it on the carpet and we started going through the pictures. It was fun. We'd not looked at them for ages.

Our wedding photos were in there. We looked so young in them! It was odd to see ourselves without kids. Many of the London crew were at the wedding, and some of our university mates came too. It was interesting to think of what everyone is up to now. Most couples are also married with children, though a few have split up. Others we've not seen for years. The pictures were like a snapshot of our lives at that moment, when we decided to tie the knot. It seemed so long ago.

We went through various packets of mixed-up photos. There were some school snaps that I'd taken with my first camera. I only know one or two people from those days, though I've recently been in touch with a few people on the Web. There were some great university pictures from our first year together. They reminded me of what an exciting carefree time that was. We looked so happy.

It was good to look at the pictures together, over wine, and remember those early days. Maybe we can feel something like that again? Maybe we can fall back in love? We may be finally making positive steps in that direction. Sorting out our sex life might be the key; it can put such a strain on things.

Near the bottom of the box of bygone memories was a packet of photos from our Ibiza trip, back in the 90s. They were hilarious! There was a classic one of Jason, Alex and myself on the beach, looking dead white and skinny, and some of us visiting various sights in our clapped out hire car. It looked like 28 years ago instead of 18.

As we neared the end of the pack I knew what was coming...It was the second from last picture. I studied it for a while, with Fiona looking over my shoulder. There she was, wearing a pair of high-cut, white bikini bottoms, with her fantastic gravity-defying tits on show. She had a short bob haircut and was sporting a pair of rather tacky sunglasses. She was grinning from ear to ear. I'd forgotten how fabulous her body was back then. She'd have given a Scarlet a run for her money. I turned to Fiona. She was smiling, as if she knew what I was thinking. "Wow" I said. "Way to go girl!"

Fiona and I chatted excitedly about our possible holiday plans for next year. We agreed to go somewhere in the Med—perhaps Greece, Spain or Italy. Turkey is also meant to be nice. A family beach holiday would be fun, with a bit of culture thrown in. My promotion means that we can probably afford one. It's going to be excellent. I asked Fiona, half jokingly, if she'd go topless again. "Would you like me too?" she replied. I looked at the picture and nodded. "OK, if you like" she replied, smiling.

I was completely knackered by ten. The two late nights in a row had worn me out. We'd also polished off a bottle of wine between us. I went to bed while Fiona stayed up a little longer, watching TV.

I only half remember her coming up and getting in beside me.

Saturday
39 years, 364 days

Despite the kids waking up at an ungodly hour and jumping on us, I can't remember a nicer Saturday morning for the longest time. I felt very content.

I gave Suzy and Michael their breakfast and prepared some eggs on toast for myself. I nearly always have eggs on Saturday mornings. There's not enough time during the week, so it's my weekend treat. I often listen to the radio, watch a bit of TV or look at stuff on the Web, while I munch on my breakfast and drink a coffee. I kick back for an hour or so in my dressing gown, content that I don't need to rush to the station, travel up to London on that fucking train with the rest of the depressed inhuman cunts, and spend the day at the office. Just knowing that I have two days off from all that shit—or three in today's case—lifts my sprit immensely.

Of course there's always a lot to do at weekends. That's why I make sure that I enjoy Saturday morning before the madness begins. Mindful that the weekend ahead was going to be a particularly busy and eventful one, I grabbed a pen and paper to write down some things that needed doing for the party. There was quite a list.

Fiona came down. She'd showered. She joined me at the table and added a few items to the to-do list. We discussed food arrangements and agreed that a barbecue would be a good idea. We needed to go shopping.

Once I'd dressed and Fiona was busy getting the kids ready, I headed to the garden shed to look for the barbecue. It was 10:15 am and the sun was already high in the cloudless blue sky.

We've not used the garden much this summer. I was so convinced that we weren't going to get the chance, that I'd already put the chairs and table away. I got them out again, then retrieved the barbecue. It'd not been used since last Bonfire Night and was full of spent charcoal and fossilised meat, that had fallen between the grating in the dark. I started to clean it up, until Fiona announced that she and the kids were ready to leave.

We drove Suzy to her dance lesson in the next town, then spent an hour at the nearby supermarket, getting most of the stuff that we need for Sunday–burgers, bangers, chicken drumsticks, fish, buns, salad, ketchup, relish, beers, wine and pop. We sat Michael in a trolley and whizzed around the store, filling it up. It wasn't cheap. But it looks like quite a few people could be coming tomorrow, so we don't want to run out of food or drink.

As we headed back to the car with our shopping, Fiona stopped to admire a dress in the window of a department store. She admitted that she didn't know what to wear tomorrow. I suggested that we went back to take a look at it after we'd picked up Suzy.

Suzy loves to dance. It's too early to tell whether she has a talent in that department, but she certainly enjoys it. She takes two consecutive classes on a Saturday morning–tap then ballet. Seeing her dance is a joy to behold! She's a lesson in concentration, but every now and then she catches a glance of Fiona or I watching her through the window and she breaks into a shy smile. We made it back in time to catch the last minute or so of her ballet.

Back at the store, Fiona went to try on the smock, while the three of us waited on the comfy chairs outside the changing rooms. It was a knee-length summer-dress with an open neck, made of white cotton, with a yellow floral pattern on it, and a belt fashioned out of the same material. She emerged from the cubicle and gave us a twirl. It looked fabulous! I'd not seen in her in a pretty dress for ages. I guess that's because she hasn't worn one, as we don't often go out these days. She loved it too and the kids also approved, so I offered to buy it for her. It was in the end of summer sale. She was very pleased.

I went in search of something for myself, while Fiona looked at underwear. I'm not a fan of shopping, so as soon as I see something half decent that is relatively cheap, I take it. In this case I found a short-sleeved Hawaiian-style shirt. I already have some shorts and flip-flops that I bought at the start of the summer and have not really used, so that was my outfit sorted for the party.

I found Fiona and the kids in the hosiery section. I always feel a little uncomfortable among the huge bloomers, tights and heavy-duty bras–it reminds me of going shopping with my grandma when I was a kid. But a pair of knickers on a mannequin caught my eye. They were the kind of skimpy underwear that I imagine Scarlet, Lucy, or perhaps Annette might wear—a tiny, sheer triangle of fabric with a string at the back. I pointed them out to Fiona. She raised her eyebrows and laughed. Then realising that I was serious, she asked me "Really?" I nodded.

She grabbed a pack of regular knickers, then after some deliberation, and further encouragement from me, she took one of the micro G-strings as well. I was very pleased. I can't wait to see her in it.

We arrived back home eager to get started with the preparations for tomorrow. But no sooner had we unloaded the food and drinks from the car than I received a rather alarming text. It was an automated message from the Fire Emergency Response Team at work, notifying me about an incident. Geoff must have already put my number on the system. I'm not expected to be on call until I've done the training course, but I immediately recognised the address listed on the alert—it was the Nestors'!

There were no details on the nondescript message, so I had no idea of how bad the fire was. I didn't have Geoff's number to call him, but I knew that I needed to go down there. The Nestors' house is one of my jobs; there'd not been a fire at one of my jobs before. It worried me. I wanted to know what had happened—whether the system had worked, what the damage was like, and whether the Nestors were OK. It was personal. I had to go.

I broke the news to Fiona. She seemed disappointed; she had something planned for the afternoon, a surprise, though she couldn't tell me what. I promised that I'd be no more than a couple of hours. Then I tore off in the car.

The roads were busy. People were taking advantage of the warm weather and the bank holiday weekend. I quickly realised that it was going to take me more than a couple of hours to get there and back. I followed the ring-road around to Kent and headed into Greater London that way.

I still had no idea of what had happened. My mind flipped between the extreme scenarios of a completely burnt-out building and a minor incident that'd set off the sensors.

As I finally pulled into the Nestors' mansion and through their open gates, it was clear that it had not been a minor incident. Two fire engines were parked on the drive, along with a police car and an ambulance. My heart sank.

Other than the mass of emergency vehicles and a few personnel, there was however, little evidence of any damage. I spotted Geoff talking to a policeman. "Thought I'd better come" I explained, approaching him. "Good man...Follow me" he replied, finishing his conversation and leading me around the house. We passed through the side gate, stepping over several giant fire hoses laid across the path, and emerged at the back of the Nestor's abode, where the action had taken place. There were five or six fire crew, another policeman, two medics and the Nestors themselves. I breathed a sigh of relief.

"Type A, possibly C" Geoff informed me, pointing to the upper floor of the building, where the damage was now clearly visible. "Probably a small appliance" he continued, "Fire services were here pretty quick...Sprinklers dealt with the bulk of it. Though one room's gutted." I recognised the smashed, smoke-blackened window as that of Natasha's dressing room, adjacent to the master bedroom.

We continued across the lawn and met Nial, another member of the Fire Emergency Response Team. He was wearing one of the company's fluorescent tabards, over a t-shirt, shorts and trainers, as if he'd been enjoying the sunny weather before he was called out to the fire. "Welcome to the old FERTs!" he joked, thrusting out his hand.

I already know a fair bit about of our fire response operations. Nine times out of ten there's little to do, except be on hand to advise the fire crew about the premises and it's installations, and answer questions from the client. The difficult bit is the paperwork that needs to be filled out in the days and weeks following an incident. Most of it's to cover our backs, and for the client's insurance claim.

A member of the fire crew emerged from the house and approached us. "Hair straighteners" he announced, apparently referring to the cause of the fire. Geoff tutted.

I walked over to where the Nestors were gathered, on their rattan sun loungers. Two paramedics were assisting them. Natasha was visibly upset. Her eye make-up had run down her cheeks and she was repeating something in Russian. I wasn't sure whether she was hurt, or in shock...or whether she was just upset that her designer dress and shoe collection had gone up in smoke. She'd insisted that we didn't install sprinklers in her wardrobe, so the contents would surely have been destroyed.

Clive Nestor sat beside her with Cupcake. The two of them were wet, but seemed otherwise

OK. On seeing me approach, he stood up, took a step forward and grabbed my hand with both of his. "Thank you very much" he said, shaking my hand vigorously. "You're welcome" I replied, a little surprised. "No. *Really. Thank You!*" he reiterated, with great sincerity.

He'd been out when the fire started, but returned to find the alarm sounding and Natasha in a state. Cupcake was in her bedroom, on the upper floor, so he dashed upstairs and down the main corridor, past the blazing room. Luckily the sprinklers had been activated, preventing the fire from spreading from its source. The suppression system that I'd insisted on had done its job; it'd bought him crucial time and allowed him to get to his daughter. He knew it, and he was very grateful.

I was rather taken back by Clive Nestor's reaction. He was unusually humble. I'd not expected it from him. It was a stark contrast from Tuesday, when he'd barely given me the time of day.

I warmed to Clive a little at that moment. I realised that despite being filthy rich and privileged, he *is* human after all. He probably worries like the rest of us—about his family, about his property, about the stability of his plush life. It can all disappear in an instant. I guess he realises that too.

My phone rang. It was Fiona. I'd been two and a half hours already. She seemed impatient. It was going to take me at least an hour to get back, perhaps more, so I apologised to Geoff and Nial and left the Nestors' place. There wasn't much I could do anyway. I asked whether I could help next week, with the report. It would be a good introduction to the process and I also wanted to find out more about what had happened. Geoff agreed that it was a good idea.

I reflected on the incident during my journey back. I was still in shock...I've spent so many years designing and installing fire safety systems, yet I rarely get to witness them in action. Seeing the Nestors huddled together in their garden, on such a beautiful day, distraught and unable to re-enter their house, really brought it home. They'd been lucky to get out alive. Thousands of others perish each year—burnt to death in their beds or overcome by smoke inhalation, trying to get out of the house. The sort of people who can't afford a state-of-the art water-mist system, heat sensors, door-guards or a dedicated emergency response service.

To have played a part in protecting other people's property and saving life, even that of a disproportionately rich family like the Nestor's, gives me a sense of pride and achievement that I've not felt in a while. Perhaps I *do* have a worthwhile job after all? Perhaps my monotonous daily grind *does* make some positive contribution to society? Maybe I'm *not* just wasting my life away for nothing?

I dwelled on this positive thought as I made my way back around London and up into Essex. I was glad that I'd responded to the alert, even though it'd interrupted a pleasant Saturday afternoon with the family. I'd been looking forward to getting stuck into preparing for the party. I'd also been excited about Fiona's new G-string. It popped into my mind once more as I turned into our road.

As if one shock wasn't enough for one day, I arrived back to find an unfamiliar car occupying our drive. I parked on the road and went to investigate. As I approached the house, the front door opened and there stood my Dad, holding Michael. Suzy appeared from behind his legs and shouted "Surprise!" I was still a little numb and detached after the Nestors' incident, and spending an hour in the car, on my own, so seeing my parents was absolutely the last thing I'd expected, especially as I'd spoken to them in France less than 24 hours earlier.

It was a lovely surprise of course, but it took me a fair few minutes and a cup of tea to adjust to what was going on. They explained that they'd been planning on coming over all along. Fiona knew, but was keeping it a secret. They're staying at their flat in London and are coming to the party after all. I'd already accepted that they were going to snub me on my 40th. I had no idea that it was a wind-up.

Fiona and Mum had made some progress preparing for tomorrow. They'd marinated the chicken and cooked a few small dishes. Dad had also made himself useful while they'd waited for me by cleaning the barbecue that I'd left in the middle of the garden. Suzy and Michael had helped him. It was cute to see them together. Mum and Dad love the kids. They also think the sun shines out of Fiona's arse.

It was still warm in the garden at dinnertime, so we decided to eat outside. I'd never have expected that it'd be possible a few days ago. The summer had seemed dead and buried. We sat catching the last of the sun's rays before it disappeared over the neighbours' houses.

Mum and Dad filled us in on life over in France. They live in a pretty rural area, so not a lot happens. Mum insinuated that things between

Margaret and Xavier are still not great. I didn't fish for any details. Margaret met him while he was a chef at a London restaurant. After a couple of years together, they moved abroad to open a guesthouse. We've been there on holiday several times—mostly because we can stay for free. The weather is usually better out there, but it's quite far inland and there's not a lot to do. I don't know how she's put up with living there for so many years. It's got to be partly to blame for their marital problems.

Mum and Dad moved over to keep Margaret company. They fell in love with a run-down farmhouse in the same village and decided to buy it. Margaret had had two kids by then and they'd not seen much of them, so it made sense. Dad had just retired, so the renovation kept him busy, for the first couple of years at least. Mum reinvented herself as chic Euro-pensioner—cycling around the village and hanging out with her other ex-pat friends. Margaret clearly enjoys having them over there, especially Mum, though I don't reckon Xavier is too keen on his in-laws living so close. This might be another source of friction between him and Margaret.

It got a little cold outside once the sun had left the garden, so we moved back into the house. Dad and

I put the kids to bed. They both lay in Suzy's bed, with the light off while Dad gave them a bedtime story. He was always good at telling stories when I was a kid. He just made one up off the top of his head. The kids loved it. Michael fell asleep almost immediately, so I carried him into his own bed.

We drank tea with Mum and Dad, down in the kitchen, as they got ready to leave. They asked me about the promotion, so I filled them in on my presentation and the interview–though I didn't mention Twatface. Dad seemed pretty pleased for me and maybe even a little proud for once. He always reckoned that I'd not made proper use of my 'university education'. One of his childhood friends has a son of the same age, who went on to become a barrister. Dad used to bring this up during arguments, which didn't exactly do wonders for my self-confidence. It's always nice to get his approval. It means a lot.

Mum and Dad left around 9:30pm and drove back up to London in their hire car. They offered to return early in the morning to help with the party preparations, but I said that we had it under control. It'd been good to see them, but Fiona and I need a bit of space to get things in order.

We sat down and compiled an almost final guest list for tomorrow. Most people had replied either way, but there were still a few maybes. The list included: Jason and possibly Luther, who he's now invited; Nick and Vanessa and their teenage son; maybe one of my original raving pals Steve, who I've not seen for years; local couple Giles and Maria with their daughter Sophie, from Suzy's class at school; Fiona's friend Jackie, who also lives in the village; Clare and maybe Mark from work; Mum and Dad...That's 16 bodies if everyone comes. The house is going to be full. If a few people don't turn up then we're still guaranteed a good crowd. We were both excited.

As we went to bed, still discussing arrangements, it occurred to me that it's my birthday tomorrow. I'd almost forgotten, amidst all the excitement, what the party is in aid of. It'd been a busy and eventful last day, of a busy and eventful last week.

I feel a little nervous that I'm just one night's sleep away from the main event. The week's gone pretty quickly. Have I made sufficient use of it?...I've certainly achieved a lot and I've thought a fair bit. I've realised some things about myself and straightened out a few aspects of my life. But am I really ready? Am I ready for the big four-zero?

I don't know. I'm certainly more ready than I was on Monday. But I guess I'll never be ready. I don't particularly want to get older. I don't exactly relish leaving my 30's behind and running up the clock towards 50–because that's what's going to happen. Next year I'll be 41, then the digits will just flit away 'till I'm staring at the next psychological milestone approaching on the horizon.

It's pretty damn close now. There's no more time to dwell on it. Ready or not, it's time to take it on the chin.

Sunday
39 years, 365 days

The last day of my 40th year on planet Earth began with a massive family cuddle. I couldn't think of a nicer way for it to start. Fiona and the kids brought me cards and presents in bed. It was cute to think that they'd made them at some point in the week, then stashed them away somewhere 'till my birthday. The kids were very excited as I opened their creations—a card with crêpe-paper flowers from Suzy, written in her neatest joined-up handwriting, and an abstract painted effort from Michael, which he proudly announced was a "fi-a-ren-gin."

Fiona had bought me, or more precisely us, a weekend break to Paris. As I opened the envelope, which contained train tickets and a hotel voucher, she explained that "It would be good for us to get away. Just the two of us." I nodded in agreement, while reading the card. "I've already asked Jackie to look after the kids" she added. It was a lovely gesture. I was really taken back. I'd expected a book, or maybe some aftershave.

Fiona shepherded the kids downstairs to give them their breakfast. I closed my eyes and prepared for a snooze, but she reappeared a few minutes later, closing the bedroom door behind her. "I've put them in front of the telly, with some toast" she explained. I smiled, expecting her to get back in bed beside me for a lay-in. Instead, she reminded me that she'd still not given me my surprise. She was of course referring to yesterday—she'd had something planned for me, before I ran off to the Nestors'.

She disappeared into our bathroom and seemed to be having a shower. The door opened a little later and Fiona came back out...She was wearing the new knickers that I'd bought her, and nothing else. They looked truly microscopic, barely covering her crotch, with the string biting into the skin around her waist. She stood there, in the middle of the bedroom, with her hands on her hips, as I checked the panties out.

I don't often study Fiona naked these days; she's not got the body that she used to have and I must admit that I sometimes avert my eyes when she is dressing or undressing. I didn't look away this time. Instead, I feasted my eyes on her. I enjoyed her. I tried to look past the wobbly bits that I'm normally scared of and focus instead on her good points—her tits, her legs, the ultra skimpy knickers. She smiled back. I started to get a hard-on.

Fiona then approached the bed and asked "D'you want to see your surprise then?" I was even more confused. If my parents coming over yesterday wasn't the surprise and the knickers weren't either, then what was it that she had to show me? She smiled again, then looked down at her nether regions and her almost see-through underwear. I then twigged what is was...My knob went rock hard and my heart began to beat faster.

I crawled to the end of the bed where Fiona was standing. I grasped her knickers and slowly pulled them down...revealing her clean-shaven pussy. It was definitely a surprise; I'd not expected her to grant my wish so soon. I was taken back by the sight of it, and paused to take a closer look. I'd not seen her without at least a modest covering of hair. It was as if a part of her was missing; which of course it was.

Noticing the inquisitive look on my face, Fiona asked "D'you like it?" I nodded. "Really?" she enquired. "Yes. I like it a *lot*" I replied. She looked happy that I'd approved. She then asked, somewhat shyly "Do you want to lick me?"

I'd not gone down on her for years. We'd stopped having oral sex at some point after the birth of Suzy. It just wasn't on the menu anymore. But remembering my blow job on Thursday night, I felt as if the time had come to get to know her pussy again...So that's what I did.

I'd forgotten how sexy it feels to be pleasuring a woman with my tongue; to be getting close and personal with her most private of areas. The absence of hair made it feel as if I was in a porn movie.

Fiona seemed to enjoy it too. She eventually started moaning, so I stopped, rolled her on her side and got into her from behind. She was so wet that I slid in effortlessly. I reached around and felt her bare crotch with my hand, as I moved in and out of her—slowly, gently, but passionately. The only audible sounds were the birds outside, the slightest hum from the TV downstairs and Fiona's gentle sighing.

Her breathing gradually quickened as she began to climax. I put my finger in her mouth to stop her screaming. She sucked on it and let out a deep moan through her nose instead. This set me off. Moments later I came like I've never done before, fighting to stop myself belting out an obscenity. It was like peaking on some amazing euphoric drug. For a second or two I was in heaven, experiencing the purest, most natural high known to man.

As it subsided and I caught my breath, I reflected to myself that this is how it is meant to be— great sex; no inhibitions; Fiona and I in sync with one another. It was birthday sex of the sweetest variety. What a way to start the day!

There were more birthday cards on the table at breakfast. Fiona had been saving them for me during the week. I opened a few while the kids looked on with interest. One was from my aunt and uncle, another from the neighbours, who I'd forgotten to invite to the party, and one was from Margaret, Xavier and family. It looked certain that she wouldn't be coming, which is fair enough given the distance, and her commitments with the guesthouse. Mum and Dad were probably enjoying the weekend away from her. I haven't spoken to Margaret in several months, so it was nice to get a card from her.

I went straight round the neighbours' after breakfast and told them about the party. It was lovely outside—the birds were singing and bees were buzzing around the flowers in their front garden. The sustained good weather has really brought things back to life. It felt like mid-summer, not the tail end of August.

Anthony was in the garage, cleaning his motorbike. He looked up over his glasses and smiled when I knocked on up-and-over door. "Looking good!" I commented, nodding at his shiny ride. "She's a beauty, hey?" he replied.

I thanked him for the card and invited him to the party. He said that they'd love to come, but he'd check with Barbara first, who was out.

Jason was coming round at noon to set up his music and help with the preparations. I'd successfully put off Mum and Dad until 2:00pm, when the party was due to begin. I dressed in my new shirt, shorts and flip-flops, then got on with re-arranging the kitchen and setting up the garden. Fiona was busy upstairs getting the kids bathed.

I then wandered into the village to buy a few things that we'd forgotten yesterday—tonic water, limes, firelighters, candles. It was now truly glorious outside. It reminded me of birthdays of old, when I was a kid. I mostly remember them being sunny. I'd play in the garden with my new toys or have a friend or two around. Perhaps I look back at those days with rose-tinted glasses, but recent birthdays just haven't been as special.

As I strolled into the village, I felt that joy once more; that sense of importance and expectation. It was *my* day—*my* day to enjoy and to feel special. People were giving up *their* day to celebrate with me. The weather was also shining favourably on me after a damp, shite summer. All my cares and worries about becoming 40 had evaporated into the warm mid-morning air.

I shopped for supplies along the High Street, in an upbeat mood. People were wandering about in the sun, browsing the small strip of shops, pubs and other businesses, or running errands. It was pretty idyllic. This is one of the benefits of living outside of the metropolis. You can't get that village atmosphere in London, unless you're rich enough to live in Hampstead or Notting Hill. I need to enjoy it more often and try to shop locally, instead of using the supermarket in the next town.

I must've been smiling when I paid for my stuff in the grocery shop, as the Indian woman, who runs it with her husband, commented "Lovely day today." I looked out of the window of the dark, cramped store, between the assortment of handwritten advertisements for cleaning services, second-hand bikes and puppies for adoption, at the bright midday sun. "Yeah, it is" I replied, "It's my birthday…I'm 40." "Oh, well, happy birthday to you" she said, perhaps a little surprised. It didn't feel odd or shameful to admit my age. I didn't feel particularly older at that moment. I felt relaxed and decidedly positive. I suddenly felt like embracing my age, not denying it. That way it might not get the better of me.

I ambled the half a mile or so back home, through the bustling park, past Suzy's empty school and into our street from the other end. As I neared the house, a beat-up blue hatchback swung into the road and honked its horn at me. It was Jason.

He pulled up beside the kerb and stuck his arm out to offer me a high-five. "Happy birthday my son!" he chirped. He was smoking and his car was full of fumes. On the back seat was a profusion of equipment and boxes of records. "You brought decks?!" I enquired, noticing a pair of turntables stacked on top of one another. "Yes indeed!" he replied, "And lots of old tunes."

I helped Jason unload the contents of his car into the house, then I showed him around the place.

He'd not yet been down to Essex to see us, so I was keen to give him a tour of our rural retreat. "It's huge!" he commented. It's not exactly a mansion, but it must seem gigantic compared to our poky old flat in London.

Fiona had been laying out stuff for the party while I was in the village—glasses, plates, cutlery, plastic bowls and cups for the kids. She'd also put up some decorations, including a banner that read '40 Years Young Today!'. I opened the patio doors and took Jason into the garden. The cat was laying on the lawn. "Nice…I'd love to have a garden" Jason said. It's not much more than about 30 square meters of grass, that I have to painstakingly weed, cut and clear of leaves throughout the year, but on a summer's day it's perfect.

We moved back inside the house and went upstairs. I called for Fiona, in case she wasn't decent, but there was no reply. The kids were in Suzy's room. They'd been bathed and were dressed. Jason hadn't met Michael before. He bent down, shook his little hand and started to chatting with him. Michael was driving his toy cars along the patterned rug on Suzy's floor, pretending that it was some sort of highway. Jason sat down and joined him. I'd forgotten how great he is with kids.

Suzy was dressing and undressing her Barbies. I asked where Mummy was. "She's in the bathroom" replied Suzy, "Doing ladies stuff." I gathered that she was getting herself ready, so I sat down with Jason and the kids and joined in with their game.

A few minutes later, across the hall, our bedroom door opened and out came Fiona. She was in her new summer dress and a pair of high heels. Her hair was styled, she was wearing little pendant earrings, and she had lipstick on. She looked positively radiant as she approached Michael's open door. From our sitting position on the carpet, she seemed a foot or so taller in her high heels, like some long-legged femme fatale.

"Hi Jason!" she said, suddenly noticing him, among the toys. "Hello Fi" he replied, looking up at her and smiling, as she paused in the doorway. "You look lovely" he commented, beating me to it. "Thank you" she replied, shyly. "It looks amazing on you" I added, referring to the dress. She stood up straight and turned slowly around, showing it off, to Suzy's delight.

I'd not seen Fiona looking so beautiful in a long time. I felt a rush of pride seeing her standing there, and noticing Jason's reaction. They'd not met for several years, so I was happy that he witnessed her looking her best.

I realised that I *do* still fancy my wife after all these years; that I *can* still appreciate her beauty, despite living with her day in day out for nearly two decades. In that time I've seen her dog-tired and haggard; white faced, covered in sick and puking her guts up over the toilet bowl; I've watched her get pregnant twice, then seen her give birth; I've studied her body from every angle and spotted imperfections that even she didn't know existed; I've watched her slowly deteriorate over the years from the sprightly, spring chicken that I kissed one night at university, into a slightly above average pre-middle age mother of two.

After witnessing all this, it's perhaps not surprising that my desire for her has waned somewhat and that I sometimes find it hard to recognise her good points. But seeing her standing there, in her new dress, looking happy, confident and excited about the party, it came back to me. I saw a flash of youth in her smiling face—a radiance that I recognised, but which I often forget about. It was shining through at that moment.

Fiona definitely feeds off my vibes and off the current state of chemistry between us, so the positivity that I've discovered this week and the way in which we've reconnected with each other might also be giving her a new lease of life. I could see it in her smile and in the way she was holding herself....Jason was right; she *did* look lovely, and at that moment I felt very proud to think that she's mine.

We tended to a few last minute things while Jason set up his turntables on the patio, on an old paint-splattered table from the shed. I brought down the hi-fi and connected it to Jason's set up.

The sky was literally cloudless. It had to be at least 30 degrees in the garden, beyond the shade of the house. I'd loaded as much beer, wine and soft drinks into the fridge as possible, to chill it down for the party.

I opened two beers as Jason put an old house classic onto one of his decks to test out the sound-system. The crackle from the record hissed over the speakers, then *Boom*! The music kicked in, taking me straight back to our clubbing days in London. It sounded superb! We clinked bottles and listened to the rest of the track, while standing on the concrete step and nodding. I could tell it was going to be a great party. Now we just needed some guests.

The first people arrived at 2:00pm on the dot–Mum and Dad. Their sudden, unexpected appearance yesterday had been such a surprise that I'd almost forgotten that they were in the country. They were followed shortly afterwards by Anthony and Barbara from next door, who didn't exactly have far to travel. They'd met Mum and Dad once or twice before, in the drive or over the garden fence that separates our houses. Being the oldest couples that we'd invited, I'd expected them to have a lot in common, but they didn't gel particularly well. The neighbours have to be in their mid fifties or thereabouts, so I guess they're a generation younger than Mum and Dad.

No one else turned up for another 20 minutes or so and I got worried that it would just be us, my parents and Ant and Babs, with Jason and his records. It would *not* have been a great party.

Luckily, several other guests appeared at the door soon afterwards. My old uni pal Steve came as promised and brought his wife Laura with him, who'd I'd not met before. They'd driven up from Brighton. It was really odd to see him walking up our drive, after so long.

I'd hardly gotten a chance to say hi and meet his spouse, when the next car pulled up on the already cramped kerb outside the house. It was

Nick, Vanessa and their son Max. They knew Steve from Leicester, so I left them to catch up with one another, while I welcomed Fiona's friend Jackie. She'd walked over from the other side of the village, holding a cake that she'd baked. Giles, Maria and Sophie then arrived, also on foot.

The house was decidedly livelier with the addition of seven more adults and two children. It seemed more like a party than fifteen minutes earlier. Fiona was serving drinks to the new arrivals and everyone seemed to be getting on OK. It was time to fire up the barbecue.

The garden was absolutely glorious. Suzy and Michael were outside, already playing with the other kids. Max was kicking a ball around with Michael, who was trying to grab it with both hands. Jason was sorting through his records and came over to suggest that he should start playing. I agreed.

He slipped a soulful, downbeat tune on and the garden filled with music. It mingled with the smell of charcoal and lighter fluid. I grabbed a beer and got to work on the cooking. It was going to be far too hot to grill in the middle of the yard, so I dragged the barbecue onto the patio and set it up against the outside wall, the other side of the sliding doors from Jason's sound-system. There we both stayed for the next hour, with a bucket of ice-cold beers between us—me flipping burgers, prodding sausages and trying not to burn the chicken, and Jason selecting one funky record after another from his box.

Despite being lumbered with the cooking duties at my own party, it was nice chatting with Jason and the other guests, who to-and-fro'ed between the kitchen and the garden. I filled him in on Friday, my promotion and TF's no-show. "Did I hit him that hard?" he enquired. "It was a pretty gruesome shot" I replied, laughing. I still found it very funny, though part of me hoped that Jason and I had only bruised TF's ego and that there would be no repercussions next week at work.

I filled several trays with sticky, sizzling meat and fish, then set them on the kitchen table, beside Fiona's pre-prepared dishes, so people could tuck in. They must have been hungry, as there was a sudden rush to eat. I was hot and sweaty, so I left them to it and headed upstairs to freshen up a bit.

On my way back down, the front doorbell rang. We'd propped the side gate open, so the remaining guests could just follow the noise and smell around the back to the garden. I opened the door to find Clare, standing on the step, smiling and holding a present. She had lots of make-up on and was wearing a short, sassy black dress and heels. I was quite taken back by how good she looked. I'd not seen her so done up before—it was a total transformation. She leant forward to offer me a kiss on the cheek, then handed me the present and wished me a happy birthday. I led her into the kitchen, got her a drink then began introducing her to the others, who were mostly outside, eating and chatting.

Fiona clocked her immediately and looked a little perturbed, so I took Clare straight over to greet her. They'd met once before, a few years back. I could tell from Fiona's face that she was a little put out by Clare's arrival. She'd already gotten many compliments about her new outfit and she didn't want anyone stealing the limelight. Clare's fantastic bare legs looked all the more luscious in her tight black dress, which clung to her wiry body. She'd really dressed to impress, and she *knew* that she looked great. I held Fiona's hand to reassure her, while she and Clare exchanged pleasantries. Behind them, Jason was looking over at me and mouthing "Who's that?!" I introduced him to Clare next and left them talking.

I finally got a chance to catch up with Steve, who'd been chatting to Nick and Vanessa the whole time.

They weren't exactly good friends at Leicester, but they were in the same year and have a few mutual acquaintances, such as Fiona and I. Steve was one of my main raving pals back then, whereas Nick and Vanessa were a more straight-laced couple, that Fiona got to know. I distinctly remember Nick making jokes about Steve and I, heading off to raves in Leicester city centre in our coloured jeans and fluorescent t-shirts. It was as if we'd been in some sort of secret cult, from which they were excluded—which was of course part of the attraction. Nick's quite trendy these days. He was nodding his head to the music that Jason was spinning. It's funny to think that he used to mock us like that.

It was great to reminisce with Steve about our antics two decades earlier. He gave me a short summary of his life since then. Some of it I knew already—that he'd stayed in Leicester for a few years after uni, working in a pub; that he'd then moved to London and met Laura; that they'd bought a house in Brighton and had two kids. His story was much like mine. He's now a finance administrator with the local council. He also admitted to being rather bored by his job.

I wasn't too impressed with Laura—though to be fair, I never got a chance to speak to her properly. I just didn't get a good vibe off her. Steve mentioned that she'd recently turned 40 herself. She definitely looked it. What struck me was her extremely poor attire. She was dressed in corduroy jeans, tatty loafers and an unflattering baggy shirt. It was the sort of outfit that some mothers wear to pick up their kids from Suzy's school; not what you'd choose to put on if you were attending a party on a summer's day. She looked like someone with very little pride in herself, or perhaps lacking in confidence, or maybe both? She wasn't wearing any make-up as far as I could see, and her dry, greying hair was rather unkempt. I compared her to Vanessa, who was standing a short distance away and is always well dressed. The difference was striking.

Jason announced that Luther was at the train station. He'd forgotten our address and didn't have a map, nor a mobile phone. I'd had a few beers by then, but I nipped out in the car to pick him up and bring him to the house.

Luther looked no different from the last time I'd seen him. It was hard to think that he'd had a breakdown. He seemed healthy and happy. Perhaps it was his two-year's travelling in Asia? He seemed just like his old self—chirpy, charismatic and friendly to everyone. Fiona was also very happy to see him too. It was like a mini London reunion, what with him, Jason, Fiona and I all in the same place.

With everyone in attendance and making themselves at home, I managed to have a good chat with a few other people. Dad cornered me at one point. "Happy Birthday Son" he said, resting his hand on my shoulder, "The best years are yet to come" I'd heard that old chestnut before, but never believed it. He explained that he'd really enjoyed his 40's, 50's and the first part of his 60's. They'd been more relaxed than his 20's and 30's. He'd felt more content, wiser and more in control. He'd enjoyed watching Margaret and I become adults, and make our own way in the world. He particularly loves having grandchildren, which he reckons are a completely different experience to having your own kids.

Dad offered a pretty convincing argument. It was uplifting to think that I have all this ahead of me too. It struck me that I'm only half way through my life, or maybe less? I'd been treating my 40th as the coming of old age; as if the proceeding decades will be a painful, depressing descent towards the grave. But in fact it's just the mid-point. There's a whole lot more for me to experience. I'm just entering a new phase; the next act in the story of my life.

I gleaned some very different, but equally important advice for Act II from a much younger and less experienced source—Nick. We were sitting on the garden chairs, soaking up the sun and drinking a beer, when he commented on Clare. "Would you?" I asked him, as we both looked at her across the garden in her little black number. "In an ideal world...of course" he replied.

We then got talking about sex and the temptation of other women. He reckons that he and Vanessa have always remained faithful, despite meeting at university at a similar time as Fiona and I. As far as he's aware, Fiona and I have too, at least since the Sheri business. I didn't tell him about my recent trip to the sauna.

"It's hard though" I commented, being honest with him. He nodded in agreement, then proceeded to share with me the secret behind his' and Vanessa's marital success. "Sex games" he said. I was intrigued, so I let him to elaborate. "Role-play, scenarios, fantasies..." I listened with interest as Nick argued that acting out sexy situations is the perfect way to keep things fresh in the bedroom.

I've sometimes thought about buying Fiona a costume and getting her to pretend to be a schoolgirl or a policewoman, but I've never had the balls to ask. It suddenly struck me as a great idea again. Maybe it's time to suggest it to her? Perhaps she'd be up for it? "Vanessa's great at all that" Nick went on, bragging a bit "She's always coming up with new ideas." It was almost more information than I needed to know, but I let him continue. He listed a few scenarios that they've tried–teacher giving student after-hours tuition; plumber calling round to fix washing machine; new flatmates getting to know each other over wine; chance encounter with best friend's girlfriend at the swimming pool. I particularly liked the sound of the last one.

"You can take it in any direction you want to. You just need to keep an open mind" he explained. "We once met up at a bar in town, pretending to be strangers...then spent the whole night acting out a game." I raised my eyebrows in surprise. "At a real bar?" I asked. "Yeah" said Nick "That was a great one!" I was very impressed–impressed that Vanessa is so saucy in the bedroom, but also that the two of them are prepared to go to such lengths to turn each other on. "We don't do role-play every time" he explained "But from time to time it really helps...We both love it."

I found the idea rather appealing. I spent the next half an hour or so imagining what I'd like Fiona and I to act out. I pictured her in a nurse's outfit, but with no panties or bra on. I realised that there's a whole world of sexy fun to be had; endless titillating situations that we could try out to get us in the mood for sex. I hope that she's game, because I'd love to give it a go.

The barbecue was completely out by 6:00pm and only a handful of cold morsels were left. Fiona and Mum served cake and ice cream in the kitchen. Though it was still light outside, very little sun was left in the garden, so people gradually migrated inside to grab some dessert or seek warmth. Even the kids went in, to play up in Suzy's and Michael's rooms.

I felt a little guilty that Jason had spent the whole afternoon spinning records, but I guess he's used to it. He appeared to be enjoying himself, playing all his old vinyl. People were certainly very appreciative. I suggested that he brought his equipment inside, so we unplugged it and set it up on the worktop in the kitchen. Jason reconnected it all again, while Nick and I moved the kitchen table and chairs out of the way to create a makeshift dance-floor.

We'd not long finished reorganising the kitchen and were about to get the party started again, when the lights went out. The place fell silent and I heard someone ushering the kids back downstairs. I then twigged what was going on...

Fiona appeared a few seconds later, holding a cake and singing 'Happy Birthday To You...'. Everyone joined in as she approached me, in her pretty dress, with the candlelight flickering on her smiling face. The cake, which she'd baked herself, had four candles, one for each decade of my life, and a big '40' written on the top in blue icing. People crowded around and I blew it out.

It was very touching to be surrounded by my friends and family on my birthday. I'd not expected at the beginning of the week that I would see it out in such great company.

"Make a wish" shouted Suzy...so I did. I closed my eyes and wished that the second half of my life will be as good as the first has been; that Fiona, the kids and I remain healthy and happy; that I don't let things get me down so easily; that I see past my superficial worries to see the bigger picture...which is that I am a lucky man–lucky to have a loving family, a steady job and a home to call my own; lucky that I'm not ill or disabled, that I've not lost a loved one, that I'm not homeless, penniless, alone or persecuted. Because these are real reasons to feel unhappy, trapped, depressed and ready to give up.

Mum and Dad left not long after the cutting of the cake. They fly back tomorrow night. It was so great that they'd come. It'd really made my day. I didn't get a chance to say goodbye to them properly, given that I probably won't see them for another few months. They seemed pleased with the way things are going with Fiona and I, especially my promotion. I guess they came at exactly the right time. We must've looked happy, which was hopefully reassuring given the situation with Margaret. She and I have always vied for their attention and approval. Fiona and I gave a good account of ourselves. I'm sure they'll be singing our praises. It's a nice feeling.

Mum and Dad were unusually relaxed and got on well with most of our friends. I noticed how much they appear to love each other still. They've definitely had their ups and downs in the time that they've been married, but they seem very content with one another at the moment. It was nice to watch. I hope that Fiona and I can survive that long and still respect each other, as they seem to. We've certainly got a lot to learn from them.

Anthony and Barbara also departed around the same time. I could tell that the party was not their cup of tea; they only knew Fiona and I, and the kids. It's a pity Mark never turned up. He might have gotten on with Anthony. I'd not heard from him, nor had Clare.

With Mum and Dad and the neighbours gone, Jason dimmed the kitchen lights and turned up the volume.

Jackie was the first to dance, followed by Fiona. She seemed a little relieved that my parents had left. She loves them dearly, but she can't totally relax in their presence. She poured herself a large drink and joined Jackie, who was already pretty pissed and had black teeth from all the wine she'd drunk. Vanessa and Nick appeared, then Clare, and took to the kitchen dance-floor as Jason upped the tempo and a whole different phase of the party began.

Sensing that it was now 'adults time', I took the kids upstairs and put them in their pyjamas. I stuck a film on Suzy's TV and left them in front of it. Max wasn't interested, but played on his computer game instead.

Leaving the kids room, I saw Luther coming out of the bathroom, sniffing and rubbing his nose. I knew straight away what he'd been up to. He saw the look on my face and asked if it was OK. I told him to keep it discrete and to use the en-suite in our bedroom instead. He told me that it was Jason's stuff. I might have known.

Sure enough, a short while later Jason offered me some coke. I wasn't overjoyed that he'd brought narcotics to the party, but I guess that it hadn't occurred to him. It seems that he still does the stuff most weekends. He probably needs it to stay awake and fight the boredom of playing music for hours on end. He lives in a different world. One without kids or early rises, one in which it's pretty commonplace to be snorting coke in any situation. For that reason, I didn't have a go at him. The kids were safely annexed, so I told him to be careful, especially given that Clare from my work was present. "Don't worry about her" he said, "She's already had some."..."What!?" I replied in shock.

I'd noticed Jason and Clare chatting earlier in the day. She'd been hanging out by his decks in the garden. "How comes you never mentioned her before?" he enquired. I didn't know what to answer. I guess I'd never thought of Clare as his type. She's not what you'd call ugly or unattractive; I'd certainly admired her legs on many an occasion, but I'd just thought of her as a pleasant and rather sweet woman who works under me, and does a bloody good job. But seeing her all glammed-up, and hearing that she'd taken some of Jason's superstrong chang, I realised that she's not quite the innocent girl I'd previously imagined. I could see why Jason was interested. It worried me a little.

She was dancing not far away. I looked for signs that she might be off her tits, but she seemed OK. Jackie was swaying badly though. Fiona also looked to be enjoying herself, after a few drinks. I joined them on the dance-floor and had a boogie.

I'd never danced in my own kitchen to a live DJ before, or even a CD come to think of it. It was brilliant! It was as if I was at my own private rave, surrounded by my friends.

We stomped the hell out of the laminate floor for the next hour or so, as Jason spun one classic after another—stuff that we used to listen to on old cassette tapes he'd make for us. We were singing along and throwing shapes, especially Steve and I.

I briefly closed my eyes and imagined I was somewhere other than at home in my kitchen. A euphoria came over me like I'd experienced the first time we'd ventured into a Leicester nightclub, back at university. It all came back in a flash.

This has to be the way to liven up future parties and gatherings—to host your own middle-age disco. I might have to invest in a new sound system and maybe a strobe light? If we can't go out anymore, perhaps we can party at home instead. I'll have to book Jason for my 41st, and print some flyers!

A little later, I ended up sitting on the stairs chatting to Luther, while the dancing continued in the kitchen. He's an interesting chap. He recalled some of his adventures abroad. I didn't pry as to what had made him disappear like that, but I got an insight from the stuff we spoke about.

I commented on him not having a phone, upon which he embarked on a luddite monologue about the perils of modern technology and his dissatisfaction with 21st century capitalist society. He reckons that we're all frying our brains and filling them up with useless information. It's the media's fault, and corporate business, he says. They bombard us with all sorts of shit that we don't need, from the latest throw-away gadgets, to irrelevant gossip about talentless celebrities, crap soulless music and recycled fashion trends that are currently in vogue.

Though he was coked-up and I knew he'd recently spent two years on a beach in Bali, Luther's theory struck a chord with me. I noticed the other day that everyone around me on the train was staring in silence at a hand-held computerised device of one sort of another. I too was clutching my own personal apparatus, waiting for a call, a message, or an update. It was like a retro vision of the future, from an early science fiction film; as if the whole carriage were plugged into their private electronic portal, relaying them minute-by-minute information on an whole array of urgent issues.

This was of course pretty much what was happening, except I knew that most people were just browsing the Web, checking what their friends were having for breakfast or playing some mind-numbing computer game. I stared blankly at the screen on my own device, not knowing what to look at. What was that important that I needed to crane my neck and strain my tired eyes to look at on my phone at 7:30am? What news did I not already know from the free newspapers strewn around the carriage and the electronic billboards at the station? Did I really give a toss about what my friends were having for breakfast? Why didn't I just look out the window at the countryside, instead of stacking multicoloured plastic bricks in a line?

So that's what I did. Util my phone beeped.

Luther nodded as I recounted my experience to him. "They're trying to control you" he proclaimed. "They're watching you all the time…They know where you are; who your friends are; what you like; what you dislike; what your views are, and your fantasies…They know everything about you, so long as you're connected." He was talking of course about the Web. He definitely had a point. Still, if you've nothing to hide, then you've surely got nothing to worry about? Luther had a different view on this. He advocated that I 'disconnect' as soon as possible and join the revolution, as he's done.

Though I'm not about to throw away my phone and unplug my computer just because of his drugged-up sermon, Luther did get me thinking. The relentless, pervasive nature of our 'Information Society' is certainly something that I'm a little worried about. It's a total assault on the senses that I have to deal with every day, wherever I go. I also feel for the kids of today–they're going to burn out much earlier, such is the pace of life and the expectations put upon them. They'll have to grow up so quickly in order to deal with it.

I asked Luther about his plans. Was he staying in the country or heading back out to east? He told me that he's leaving again, as soon as he's saved up enough money. He came back to give it another go with his girlfriend, but she's moved on. He's an only-child and his parents divorced and remarried years ago, so there's nothing keeping him here. I felt sorry for him, not having a place to call home, or anyone waiting in for him. Surely everyone needs a sense of belonging? Otherwise we're just alone in this world, alone and astray. This is how Luther came across. Maybe that's the way he likes it? Though perhaps not if he came back?

Maybe I'll think twice if I ever feel the urge to up and leave myself. Things would have to be very dire at home to brave it on my own, as he has.

Luther and I were snapped out of our philosophical discussion by Steve, who announced that he and Laura were leaving. I must have looked disappointed. "She's driving...and she wants to go" he explained. They'd appeared to be having a bit of a tiff for most of the afternoon. Either that or they just have very bad chemistry.

"Glad you could come" I told him, "It's been great to see you mate." "Likewise" he replied, holding out his hand.

Luther got up and started to ascend the stairs. I suspected that he might be off to do a line, so I tugged at his leg and signalled for him to take Steve with him. I was right. Luther whispered in Steve's ear. "Nice one" Steve replied, and the two of them headed up to the bathroom.

Back in the kitchen, the dancing had stopped. Laura had her coat in her hand and was saying goodbye to Fiona. I thanked her for coming and told her that we'll come up and see them in Leicester. It would be fun to visit our old haunts and hang out with Steve some more. Though I'm not exactly enamoured with her. She's seems rather needy and possessive. I don't like to see my old friend being hen-pecked like that.

We headed to the front door and waited for Steve. Moments later, he and Luther came down the stairs together, looking suspicious. "Where have you been?!" demanded Laura, glaring at him impatiently. He didn't reply. He looked at me and winked instead. Then they left.

Jason and Clare were chatting in the kitchen. He appeared to be winding down his set, now that there was no one dancing.

I couldn't find Jackie, until Nick pointed her out. She was sitting in a chair in the middle of the garden, in the dark. She was very sloshed, but still awake. She appeared to be having a reflective moment, and trying to sober up. It wasn't the first time I'd seen her like this. She and Fiona often hit the red wine round our house and Jackie ends up asleep on our sofa, or we have to bundle her into a taxi. She said that she was OK, so I left her to it. It wasn't too cold out there.

To compensate for his lack of technological gadgetry, Luther had memorised the time of the last train home. It was in half an hour. I offered him to stay and sleep on the pullout bed with Jason, but he declined. Clare also needed to get back up to London, so I went to find her. She wasn't in the kitchen anymore, nor was Jason, who now appeared to have given up on DJ'ing all together and had stuck an album on. My search took me back outside, where I found the two of them, leaning against the back wall of the house...kissing!

I was flabbergasted. I'd noticed them chatting and I knew that Jason had given her some sniff, but I'd not expected to see them necking each other. "Jason!" I blurted out, blaming it on him. They stopped snogging and looked at me. Clare seemed embarrassed. "What?" demanded Jason, frowning at me...I didn't know what to answer. I couldn't exactly tell him off while she had her arms around him. She was not, by the look of it, being forced against her will. "Err...I just wanted to say that...that the last train is leaving soon" I bumbled, by way of a response. I then disappeared inside to leave them to it.

They appeared shortly afterwards. Clare seemed to be leaving. I felt bad that I'd broken them up, but then Jason announced that he was going with her. They were hitting London and checking out a club.

Jason, Luther and Clare then hurried out of the house. "I'll come back for the car and this stuff tomorrow" said Jason, turning off his decks and holding out his hand. "Great party! Love the house! Look after Fiona, and…have a happy birthday Sunshine!" he added. "Thanks for coming, and for playing…Great set!" I told him "Please be careful with Clare. Don't damage her." He grinned at me, then dashed out, kissing Fiona and pinching her ass on the way.

I couldn't believe that one of my oldest, bestest mates had just run off with my one of my work colleagues. It was a tad worrying. But she's not quite the woman I thought she was. Perhaps she's what Jason needs? Perhaps, he's what she needs? Whod've thought it?

Nick and Vanessa were next to leave. Nick was their designated driver. He had to wake up Max to guide him downstairs and into the car.

They're a lovely family; really solid and close. I can't say I've ever seen Nick and Vanessa pissed off with one another. They've been together for years. Now that I know their secret, I'll forever imagine Vanessa dressed up as an air hostess or a french maid.

Fiona woke Jackie, who'd eventually fallen asleep in the garden and was covered with a coat. She was really worse for wear, but managed to tell Fiona that she wanted to go home. I called a cab, which came in a few minutes. We helped her into the taxi and directed the driver to her house. Jackie's a divorcee and lives with her grown-up daughter. Fiona called her, so she could help mother out at the other end. She's quite used to it.

With Jackie gone and the kids in bed, Fiona and I were the only ones left up. We both agreed that it had been a great party. We'd expected it to go on longer, but it was actually nice to have the house to ourselves again. We started clearing up some of the mess, until I noticed that it was 11:45pm. Mum had confirmed, earlier in the day, that I was indeed born a minute or two before midnight. There were only 15 minutes 'till my birthday proper; technically a quarter of an hour left of my 30's. I persuaded Fiona to stop tidying and join me for a celebratory drink.

I poured two glasses of wine and we retired to the lounge. It was quite hot inside the house, so I opened the window to the garden. I turned off the lights and we sat on the sofa in the in the dark, with silvery moonlight shining onto the carpet by our feet.

It was very peaceful after the mayhem of the party. Fiona and I sat and talked.

We reflected on the day and on the friends we'd just seen, old and new. We complimented them and criticised them in equal measures, as you do, behind closed doors–Jason's excellent music; Jackie's baking; Max playing so nicely with the younger kids; my parents looking happy and healthy; Luther looking healthy and happy; Jason pulling Clare; Luther's conspiracy theories; Laura's shabby appearance; Jackie's usual drunken antics.

We also recounted the nice things people had said–about the house; about the kids; about my promotion; about Fiona's dress.

Looking at ourselves through the eye's of our visitors and contemporaries and sizing ourselves up against our assessment of their own lives, we concluded that we're actually doing OK. We're coping fine. Yes, we have our ups and downs. Yes, we have periods when we don't appreciate each other. Yes, there are times when one or other of us probably thinks about calling it a day. But despite all this, despite the stress we are sometimes both put under, we find a way of getting through those moments. We do it for each other. We do it for the family. We do it for the greater good of something bigger and more important than ourselves and our own individual needs.

This week has been one of these periods; one of these crises. The prospect of turning 40 heightened certain concerns that I had about my life. It brought out a desperate need to reassess and readdress particular key aspects of who I am and what I do in this world–from my job and my direction in life, to my home life and my relationship.

I'm so glad I've had time to think and take stock. I'm glad that I've had the chance to take action. It's been a hectic, non-stop, physically and emotionally exhausting week. It's challenged me; it's rattled my cage; it's taken me to places and situations that I normally feel uncomfortable; it's also made me do things I'd not expected.

This last desperate week has been a blessing in disguise. If I'd not been so bothered about the approach of middle age and I'd not pinned such significance to a simple number, then perhaps I'd have allowed things to continue as they were, unchallenged and unchanged. In this respect, its been a wake up call; a slap in the face.

I now realise that age is just a number. What matters instead is what's inside a person's mind and their soul, not their body. Though I'm certainly not getting any younger and I can feel my body deteriorating, year after year, I know that I've still got some untapped reserves somewhere deep inside me; some of the energetic spirit that used to course through my veins when I was a younger man. It's there for sure, like an ancient, stagnant reservoir, buried under my tired flesh and bones. This week I've realised that it can still be reached; it can still be tapped; it can still supply me with that intoxicating elixir that they call life. It just needs encouragement every now and then.

I feel as if this could be the beginning of an exciting period for me, and for us. Sure, there will be more ups and downs ahead. Fiona and I will most probably be at each other's throats again some time soon. I'm likely find something that I hate about my new position. I'll definitely get the blues when winter comes around and the days are short. But I hope that I can deal with these things more effectively than before. I hope that Fiona and I are more respectful to each other and that I remember that my job is just that–a job, to pay the bills.

Unfortunately, I can't do anything about the depressing winter weather. I'll just have to ride that one out and wait for the summer, as I've had to this and every other year.

Sitting here on the sofa, on the cusp of middle age, in my suburban home, with my wife, sharing a glass of wine, I feel as if I'm ready to press on with my journey. I feel as if I'm ready to embrace life again. I feel as if I'm better prepared for the twists and turns ahead of me than I was a week ago. I feel as if I'm ready to look forward, not backwards.

I think I've overcome my quadrophobia.

I'm cured.

ABOUT THE AUTHOR

Shaun Quinn was born in 1972, in Adelaide, South Australia, of English and Irish parents. He grew up in Essex, England. He went to university in Sheffield, then emigrated to Switzerland and California. Shaun has authored several non-fiction books and articles. He lives by the river in Kent, England, with his wife, daughter and cat.

Like the book:
www.facebook.com/quadrophobia

Review the book:
www.amazon.com

Printed in Great Britain
by Amazon.co.uk, Ltd.,
Marston Gate.